The

HISTORIAN'S
DAUGHTER

Rashida Murphy has published her short fiction and poetry in various international and Australian literary journals and anthologies. *The Historian's Daughter* was shortlisted in the Scottish Dundee International Book Prize in 2015 and is being published by UWA Publishing in 2016. Currently she is an editor at *Westerly* and Books Editor at *Cafe Dissensus*. Rashida has a Masters in English Literature and a PhD in Writing from Edith Cowan University. After a short-lived career as a pen seller, Rashida taught ESL and Writing for several years as a tertiary lecturer. In 2016 she won the Magdalena Prize for feminist research for her thesis which includes the novel *The Historian's Daughter*. She lives in Perth with her husband and visiting wildlife.

The
HISTORIAN'S
DAUGHTER

RASHIDA
MURPHY

UWAP
UWA PUBLISHING

First published in 2016 by
UWA Publishing
Crawley, Western Australia 6009
www.uwap.uwa.edu.au
UWAP is an imprint of UWA Publishing,

THE UNIVERSITY OF
WESTERN
AUSTRALIA

a division of The University of Western Australia.

National Library of Australia
Cataloguing-in-Publication entry:
Murphy, Rashida, author.
The historian's daughter / Rashida Murphy.
ISBN: 9781742588940 (paperback)
Families—Fiction.
Australian fiction.
Perth (W.A.)—Fiction.
A823.4

Typeset in Bembo by Lasertype
Cover design by Alissa Dinallo
Printed by Lightning Source

This project has been assisted by the Australian Government
through the Australia Council, its arts funding and advisory body.

 uwapublishing

I dedicate this book to my friend Mary.

I miss her every day.

In a certain sense, all men are historians.
Thomas Carlyle

The happiest women, like the happiest nations, have no history.
George Eliot

Life is pleasant. Death is peaceful. It's the transition that's troublesome.
Matthew Arnold

Part I

Family

This is not the story he wanted me to tell.

One

The hills towered, range upon range, behind the house with too many windows and women. These hills, with their memory of forest, of deodar, oak and pine, of rivers and waterfalls. The forests were long gone, along with deer and elephants and the men who hunted and were hunted. Now, derelict trees shivered in the wind and tried to stay upright. When it rained, they bent and swayed, bent and snapped and disappeared in bundles carried on the heads of village women. And the hills grew bald and bleak and the famous caves could only be accessed after the rains stopped.

The caves and hills had always been here – legend said – here, in this exact spot, before time began, before the heroes of the Mahabharata set up camp here, before the monks carved stone Buddhas into the hills. Pilgrims peered inside and snatched up sacred earth from the entrance and marvelled at the smell and softness of it on their faces and wept. Barefoot men walked past each morning carrying orange flags to the shrine of the saint revered by both Hindus and Muslims. The Sahyadari hills. Ancient. Holy. Mystical. Thirsty. And the house resisted them with its opulent garden and many windows, immune to dust and thirst. The house with too many windows and an attic.

Why had my English grandfather chosen this desolate cantonment as his final home? Captain Roper, whose impressive moustache topped an unsmiling mouth in the photograph on his bookshelf, had not been a sensible man, according to his son the Historian, my father. Maybe Captain Roper became attached to the place he had sent so many of his men to, those pale English boys unused to the steaming multitudes of India. A large asylum for 'violent insane lunatics' subject to 'maniacal paroxysms of fury' was built for British soldiers here, so they could recover from the heat and the madness before going back to England.

I wished the asylum was still around. I would send all the aunties there – those dervishes with their dusters and dupattas and constant chatter. They made my eyes water. Mostly I didn't mind them filling our house like smoke on a winter's day. But it would be nice to have the Magician and Gloria to myself. To watch the Magician's hands as they folded, kneaded, straightened, smoothened, caressed. To breathe in Gloria's hair and skin and smell honey; her sighs when she thought she was alone.

The Historian was another matter. In an ideal world it would be possible to live without the Historian. And yet he remained an integral part of *my* world, like howling dogs and rumbling trucks and staccato horns. And shiny shoes.

'Hannah?' My sister tapped her knuckles lightly on my head. 'We're going to be late for school again. Where's your bag? Let's go – come on.'

I held Gloria's hand and waited for the bus. The highway would not come here for another twenty years. The old bus would rumble along the track that used to be a road before the monsoon washed it away. By the time we got to school, we would spill our breakfasts into the paper bags we carried. Every morning the Magician insisted we eat our masala omelettes and drink a glass of milk. This is how she loved us, so we never told her about bus-sickness.

'Gloria,' I said, 'when we grow up, we shall have a quiet house. We shall have a house with a roof that slopes and windows with white frames. We shall have cream curtains tied back with bows and a tiny kitchen where you can make masala omelettes and biryani. We'll share a room and a bed. We'll never get married and never leave each other. No room for aunties and babies and visitors. No secret rooms, okay?' We settled in the back where the jolts made us jump higher than if we sat in the front.

'Quite an antisocial little person you are,' Gloria said before burying her face in the first of three bags she would use on the trip. I patted her back and fished out my own bag in preparation.

I first met the English conquistadors in the Historian's library. It was actually his father's library, his *despicable* dead father's, but he claimed the books as if they were his. I didn't know what the word meant then, could barely say it. For a long time I thought it meant come-kiss-the-doors. I thought it meant I was supposed to kiss the doors of the library every time I entered it. I was used to kissing hands and books, especially holy books. Occasionally we had to kiss food if we dropped it on the floor. Kissing doors didn't strike me as an odd thing to do. Especially when my fingers found the manes of tigers and tusks of elephants in the dark grain – just before I kissed them.

As for the conquistadors, there were so many of them. All named in blue-and-gold books on the third shelf – forty-four names on the spines of forty-four books with pictures of men wearing fan-shaped hats on the inside cover. *The English Conquistadors of India.* Some names were familiar. Like Warren and Clive, the names of my brothers. Inside these books were other words – words like 'plunder' and 'mastery' and 'tragedy'. I understood those.

I was allowed inside the library if I helped the aunties wipe books with a soft cloth while they clattered around, gossiping and grumbling and eating. They came from Bombay to get away from their sons' nagging wives or their husbands' weary faces. 'So many rooms in your house,' they said accusingly, 'and all this clean fresh air also.' The Magician always apologised and urged them to stay longer, and the Historian brought his bushy brows together to mutter 'freeloaders' under his breath.

The aunties called me *kallo*. It was true I was darker than my sister and brothers – a throwback, they said. 'Farah,' they said to the Magician, 'did you have dark people in your family? Persians can be quite dark, no?' And the Magician neither confirmed nor denied the presence of darkness in her family, smiling when the aunties tugged my hair and cackled at my frowning face.

So I kissed the doors and the books with my brothers' names on them. The aunties wiped the shelves and said I would be a good wife to some lucky man one day if I wasn't so distracted by books. They complained about what a waste of space it was to have a library instead of a room with extra mattresses where their grandchildren could come and stay during holidays.

It wasn't until I turned seven and was able to read most words on my own, that I discovered the word 'conquistador' had nothing to do with kissing a door. *Webster's English Dictionary* said it meant 'an adventurer or conqueror, esp. one of the Spanish conquerors of the New World in the 16th century'.

Later, at school, my history teacher said that Clive, Lord Robert Clive, was a common thug who stole our country and Warren, Lord Warren Hastings, was an even bigger thug who stole jewellery from old women.

'You have a self-destructive nature,' Gloria said one morning, watching me cut strips of newspaper into fringes I would hang over the mirror in our room. I hoarded pieces of paper the way she hoarded beads and ribbons. I couldn't bear to see all that paper go to the man who came to collect old newspapers. He paid two rupees a kilo for used paper. The aunties watched him carefully, then pocketed the money, and the Magician pretended she hadn't seen them do it. They didn't know I filched some from their pile.

4

Gloria couldn't see the point of old newsprint lace but didn't tell on me either. Now she held up a shiny blue book called *Your Erroneous Zones* and told me to read it.

'It says here that you can choose how to feel. You can be in charge of your emotions. You can give and receive love without limits,' she said. 'You should free yourself, Hannah, and you might even stop having nightmares.'

'I can give love. I give love to you and the Magician. But I can't stop thinking about stuff. Like what happened to old Ghafoor. Don't you ever wonder?'

'See – that's what I mean. You don't let go. Ghafoor isn't important. He lives in your erroneous zone.' Gloria snapped the book shut and flung it away from her. From the look in her eyes, it seemed as though Ghafoor lived in her erroneous zone too. Before that he used to live near the mosque and sell *jalebis* during the month of Ramzan. Men wearing flat white caps stood patiently in a queue to collect the hot syrupy circles wrapped in newspaper to take home for the breaking of the fast. Ghafoor's legendary *jalebis* – the sizzle filled the market square like honey bees in summer. Until the night he smashed the window in the Historian's library and no one ever saw him again.

It was one of those unquiet nights that had kept me awake, listening to the house and the aunties snoring. I woke Gloria when the window rattled – nothing new; the windows shook all the time, but I was glad of an excuse to wake my sister. 'I'll kill you, Hannah. I swear I will,' she growled as she rolled out of bed at the same time as the brick smashed through the window. We clutched each other in the yellow light of the naked bulb in the passage and ran to the library.

The large black arm of the *jalebi* seller lifted the latch of the window from inside. We knew that arm. It was circled around the wrist by a thick copper bracelet, and a raised scar finished at his elbow. Gloria shouted his name and the arm withdrew. Through the window we saw an old Ghafoor shape, marooned in moonlight. The shape disappeared as we ran towards the window – a thud as he dropped to the ground. The lights came on behind us, and the Historian and the Magician were in the room, along with our brothers. We spilled outside even as the Magician tried to draw us back. Ghafoor lay on a strip of moist grass outside, cradling a bottle, snuffling, trying to stand. The Historian kicked him in the stomach three times before Clive pulled him away.

'Haramzada,' shouted the Historian, and Gloria covered my ears. The Magician lifted her hands to her mouth.

'My daughter,' Ghafoor said to the Magician as he staggered up and placed his body against the broken window. 'You have daughters – I have daughters – how is a father supposed to feel when —' he never completed the sentence because the Historian kicked him again, following with a punch to his face.

'Don't you ever wonder what happened to Ghafoor?' I called out after Gloria who had lost interest in the blue book after I mentioned the *jalebi* man. 'What he was going to say before —'

'Not listening any more – take my advice. Don't mention Ghafoor again, especially when you-know-who is around. Just read the book. It'll change your life.'

I didn't. Because words like 'guilt', 'worry' and 'approval' weren't as lush as 'subjugation', 'ardour' and 'slaughter'.

The room was dark. I wasn't supposed to be there. None of us were, but Warren said it was such a good place to hide that no one would find me, and for once I would win. I let my tall brother lift me to the top of the black wardrobe and hugged him quickly when he said, 'Shush now, and be very quiet.' Warren tapped me on my knees, smiled and tiptoed out of the room even though no one else was watching.

I sat on the top of that cupboard in my short yellow dress and plastic bangles and hummed to myself. The thought of winning my first game of hide-and-seek was incentive enough to keep me quiet, even though it was boring, sitting there with nothing to do. I looked around at the boxes, albums and curtains, and wished I had thought to bring a conquistador with me. I scratched at something on the curtains that made my fingers smell. Pigeon poop. The flap of wings outside the closed window sounded eerie, and I wondered how they could have got in. I counted to a hundred, ten times, recited all the nursery rhymes I knew and repeated the names of all my conquistadors, starting with Clive and finishing with Mountbatten. I drummed on a round brass plate, hoping Warren would hear me and come back. I knew he had forgotten.

I would be here forever. Like poor mad Rani Aunty, I would be forgotten by everyone except the Magician. But I would die here because the Magician didn't know where I was, so she couldn't bring me food. I would never go to school with Gloria again or paint her toenails. I cried and leaned over the side of the cupboard and saw the long drop to the carpeted floor. When I jumped my teeth closed over my tongue and my feet went numb. I lay on the floor, breathing in dust and blood. Then I yelled.

The Magician and Warren raced in together, with Gloria close behind. The Magician scooped me up and hushed me and took me down the narrow hallway to the room I shared with Gloria. Her eyes were shiny as she kissed my face and looked at my brother. 'This is how you look after your little sister? She could have died or broken her legs. God only knows what would have happened. How am I supposed to trust you, Warren?'

My brother held out his arms and the Magician handed me over. He looked as if he wanted to cry too. 'I'm sorry, so sorry,' he mumbled, wiping my face with his white hanky. 'I will look after you better, I promise.'

Gloria squeezed my hand and straightened my frock. My tongue throbbed and I swallowed blood. I loved them all.

The Magician wiped my tongue with cotton wool soaked in fennel water, and my brothers and sister took turns to sit with me through the long evening, dabbing the Magician's herb mixture on my aching tongue.

'*Jadugar*,' whispered the night servant, rubbing my feet and clucking when I showed her my tongue. 'Your ammi is a real *jadugar* – see how quickly she made you better? She can make bad things disappear, like *jadu* – magic. She comes from an old country, far away in the land of Fars, where fire was born and her people still have the first flame. Her people were all *jadugars* and you are very lucky. Next time, don't let your wicked brother put you on top of the cupboard. There are *djinns* in that room. Now be a good girl and try to sleep.' The servant yawned and slipped away when I turned my back on her. I counted my conquistadors again to while away the time.

I imagined Warren wearing a fan-shaped hat, instructing the Magician and the aunties to hand over all their jewellery in exchange for looking after me properly. Why hadn't my brothers been named after nice conquistadors instead of thuggish ones? Lord Warren of Hastings and Lord Robert Clive of the East India Company – charged with stealing jewels and a country. Gloria told me once we were 'Anglo-Banglos', even though the Magician was Indo-Persian because 'in this country everyone knows us by our father's heritage'. Naturally I asked a dozen questions until Gloria, yawning, told me I was lucky to have a Muslim name as well. 'When you grow up you can be whoever you want to be, but I'm always going to be stuck with the name chosen by the Historian.'

The Magician came to sit with me till I fell asleep. She folded back the sleeves of her kurta and rubbed her hands together to warm them before touching my forehead. Under her breath she hummed a song in Farsi, after a quick look at the door. She stroked my cheek. 'What am I going to do with you, little one? You attract disaster like a truck going downhill on a twisty road without brakes. And you have your whole life before you – I don't know what your brothers were thinking, leaving you like that.'

'I'm thorry, Ammi.' I didn't want Clive to be included in her displeasure. He had done no wrong. And Warren had been genuinely sorry, not like the time he dropped me from the back of his bike – he had laughed then at my tears.

'Shh – don't talk. Your tongue needs rest to heal. Quiet now. Sleep, my *bacha*. And may God love you and protect you.' She continued to hum the song she had started earlier, and I wished I understood the words. I closed my eyes as her hands stroked my face.

Two

Always that dream.

I had the dream again that night, the same dream I always had. I stood alone and still in the middle of the world, which was a round disc with blurred edges and black shadows. If I moved I would tip over into the darkness. And in the darkness, the skinny girl cried because she had no clothes. The Historian came for me as I tilted and pitched around. He was a giant with bulging muscles and a syringe that he stabbed into my arm. He gave me his horns to hold onto. Then he became a goat and nibbled at my feet and told me I had bad blood.

When I screamed, Gloria rushed to my bed and held me as I shook and sweated. She ran her fingers through my tangled curls and tried to find the ribbon that usually held my hair away from my face. We looked towards the door, expecting the Magician to stumble in, but it wasn't her shadow that fell across the arched doorway. It was the Historian's. Our father was a notoriously deaf sleeper and had been known to sleep through a prison riot once, early in his career.

Now he stood by the door and enquired, 'Is she all right? That dream again? Don't wake your mother. She's very tired tonight. It's okay. I'll stay with you till you sleep, eh, Hannah? How's your tongue? Here, let me look at it.'

Gloria slipped into bed beside me and wrapped her arms around me. 'No need,' she said. 'I'll sleep with Hannah now so she won't be scared any more. All right?'

I nodded. I did not want the Historian in my room. If I closed my eyes, I could see the horns he'd grown when he was pumping out my blood. Where was the Magician? Why did he stand there, looking as if he wanted to stay? No, don't walk towards me. Don't touch me. Don't come near. I turned my back and faced the wall, Gloria adjusting her body to let me twist around in the narrow bed.

'He's gone,' she said softly, after a while. 'You know I can't sleep here, so I'll just stay till you fall asleep, okay?'

'Gloria?' The Magician's herbs had worked their magic. My tongue felt no worse than it did when I accidentally bit it. Apart from the dream, I felt good – wide awake and ready for questions and stories.

'Hmm?'

'Is he really our father?'

'Sadly, yes.'

'How do you know?'

'Just shut up and go to sleep.'

'But why is he like this? Why did the Magician marry him? And why does Meher live with us?' I caught my sister's hand and stroked her palm, making little circles with my index finger until she giggled and snatched her hand away.

'One question at a time, you little pest.' Gloria's soft voice spoke above my ear. 'I don't know why he's like this. Maybe he was born this way. And the Magician had no choice. She had to marry him when her parents died. He must have been nice when he was younger. Meher is her cousin and she lives with us because she has nowhere else to live.'

'I think Meher is horrible. She's always watching us and I think she hates me.'

'Yes,' Gloria said, turning away from me. 'Now go to sleep or I'll make Meher come and sing to you.'

∞

My English grandfather's diaries were blue and gold like the conquistador books. Grandfather Roper's diaries were our secret, Gloria's and mine. No one else knew we read them in the afternoons when the aunties napped and the Magician sat in the courtyard with her sketchbook. Gloria giggled more than she read, and I had to be patient, prompting, nodding, laughing. She didn't like it when I asked questions.

'Many of my countrymen realise that independence for India is now inevitable,' wrote my grandfather, Captain William Boyd Roper of the British 10th Armoured Division, in 1944. 'Where do they expect us to go? This, after all, is our country too. We who have married and begat children here – how are we expected to forget that? Must we be blamed for the excesses of our forebears? Those ruinous men with their thuggish ways who gave the rest of us a bad name?'

'Do you think this is important? All this stuff about thugs and ruins?'

My sister laughed. 'That's how they talked in olden times. It's just like reading stories in a book. He made it all up.'

'But the foreigners had to leave. That really happened, didn't it? The English had to leave India, had to go back where they came from? Is that why the Historian gets upset when we say we are Indian?'

'Do you want me to read or are you just going to keep talking?' Gloria flicked her hair back, putting the diary down with a thump.

'Sorry, I'm sorry…please read…I'll keep quiet.'

Gloria cleared her throat and picked up another blue-and-gold-lettered tome. 'Let's see what 1947 looks like. That's when the Historian was born. Listen – our Billy is talking about the Mountbattens as if he knew them. "I wonder if the Lady Edwina and her friend Mr Nehru will view the disintegration of the country from their boudoir? I think the Lady Edwina has taken her husband's attempt to secure an intimate relationship with Nehru too literally." Quite a cat, wasn't he, old Grandpa Billy? Billy the *billa*.'

'Read some more.' I liked the sound of 'boudoir' as much as I did 'conquistador'.

'"The mortal coldness of the soul like death itself comes down." This one's dated the day after the Historian was born.'

I clutched her hand and hung on. 'What does it mean?'

'It's a quote from Byron – the poet the Historian's named after. See, Grandpa wrote it here – George Gordon Byron. Anyone would be grumpy with a name like that. You know the Historian was called Jordan when he was little? And I was meant to be called Jordana – thank goodness they picked Gloria instead.'

Gloria's dimples marked her cheeks and I leaned forward and kissed her face. She squealed and pushed me away. 'Now, where were we? Yes, let's see what Grandpa said next. Who can blame the Historian for thinking his old man was silly? Grandpa Billy was so morbid. He did kill himself, after all. Oh, here's another one about our dear old dad.'

'Read it, read it – please?'

Gloria tried to sound like Grandfather, whom neither of us had met. She cleared her throat and read in a deep voice, 'My boy, dark-haired, fair-faced, noisy, squalling – eminently suited for the new India, I think, with its noise and squalor. But does this India have any place for us? Does the Nehru–Gandhi coterie have a plan for the former rulers of India or is it to be a bloodbath? What is to become of us? This is our home. We have known no other and grow weary with the effort of remembering the green green grass of home.'

'Don't read any more,' I said. 'Let's look at the conquistadors.'

Gloria put the diaries away and pulled down the conquistadors one by one, showing me square black-and-white pictures on shiny paper inside the yellowing books. She pointed out Lady Edwina, elegantly gowned and sashed, standing between her handsome husband and the prime minister, who was wearing the coat that would become known as the Nehru jacket.

'Hard to imagine them being intimate,' Gloria said. 'Lord Louie is much better looking than Pandit Nehru.'

'Maybe Pandit Nehru was kind,' I said, and Gloria looked at me, snatched the book out of my hands and roughly shelved it. I straightened it, lingering over Lord Mountbatten's name on the blue-and-gold spine, glad that he didn't steal from old women, glad that he had returned our stolen country to us.

Another time, under a big pile of books in a corner of the library, Gloria found a book called *Coffee, Tea or Me*. She read it in a single afternoon, giggling and shushing me when I objected. When she finished she said she was going to be an air hostess when she grew up. She walked around the library with a couple of the conquistadors balanced on her head for poise. She was good at it, and didn't once drop the books, which was just as well. They were frayed with frequent handling, and it was only a matter of time before the Historian found out and we'd be banned from the library.

I tried to read Grandfather Roper's diaries on my own but it wasn't the same. Gloria knew where to find the most interesting bits.

'Gloria,' I whined. 'Don't do it. Don't be an air hostess. You can't walk around on high heels on a plane. It's silly. You're going to be a famous writer, or a pretty model, not a waitress. Please, please read the diaries for me.'

Gloria put on her superior face and said I wouldn't understand. I grinned and shook a bottle of nail polish, asking if I could paint her nails.

'All right,' she said, nose still in the air, stretching her bare feet out on the library floor where we sat.

It was a quiet afternoon. Most of the aunties and cousins were out on mysterious errands, and our brothers were playing badminton outside. They were supposed to be looking after us. The Magician was busy with the tailor all day, measuring the windows for summer curtains. After that, we were going to be measured for new dresses. Gloria was in a dilemma. She wanted new clothes but she couldn't stand the tailor. Abdul Master was a ratty little man with greasy hair, brown teeth and a leery laugh. The Magician thought he was worth his weight in gold. He raised our arms and circled our bodies with measuring tape, brushing his fingers over our chests and hips and stomachs while coughing up phlegm. He had sour breath and stained fingernails. I didn't like him either, but reckoned it was a small price to pay once a year for clothes that hadn't been previously worn by Gloria. We dawdled in the library with Grandpa Billy and his conquistadors, and I gathered up old newspapers to spread under our feet before the toe-painting ritual. These were rare, these moments alone with Gloria, without her noisy friends, without the Magician or the Historian, without the aunties calling us unfortunate half-breeds. Here we were – the two of us.

'How do they put the pearls inside the bottle?' I asked, looking at the drop of pink clinging to the tip of the brush.

'I don't know,' she sighed. 'I've told you, they're not real pearls. Just something they put inside the bottle that rattles when we shake it.'

I nodded and concentrated on painting first her nails, then mine, screwing the top back on between coats, shaking the pearls vigorously to release their shine. We waited for the polish to dry, repeating the process twice, then lay back on the hard floor, content. The wind drifted in through louvred windows, bringing the smell of star jasmine and carrot halva into the room. We looked at each other and twitched our noses.

'Come on, child,' Gloria said, after a while. 'Let's go and get groped by Awful Abdul. I don't understand why Ammi won't find another tailor.'

'You won't really go away to become a *Coffee, Tea or Me* girl, will you? We need to find out why Grandpa Billy killed himself. You promised.'

'Well, stop having nightmares about your father and I'll read to you again. Why are you such a morbid little creature?'

'I can't help it – the dreams. I wish I didn't have them. I don't have them when you sleep with me.'

'Hannah, you're eight years old. You're too big to sleep with me. And you kick and carry on all night. But this I can do – I can read you a nice story before you go to bed so you don't have nightmares, okay? One story every night from the Magician's Persian fairy tales, I promise.'

I lunged at her and fastened my arms around her waist, despite her screams and attempts to push me away.

Three

There were so many of us, so many relatives and strays in that large house with high ceilings and the mad woman in the attic. Aunties, uncles and cousins came and went but the mad woman stayed. As far as anyone knew she had lived in the attic before we were born, and the aunties contradicted each other about why she had been sent there.

The attic was a spooky place, with a low ceiling that sagged in the middle and the smell of dust in the old carpets. Rani Aunty was the Historian's sister and had always been locked up in the attic. I was nearly nine when the Magician allowed me to visit her. I didn't know it then, but I was the first among my siblings ever to see her.

We walked to the room, which had a brass lock on the outside. I held a tray of food and the Magician unlocked the door. It opened with a sigh. 'Now, listen, Maryam *jaan*,' she said quietly, 'don't jump on her and don't ask too many questions, okay? She's a very special lady and she is your aunty, your *real* aunty. You must be respectful.' The Magician only called me Maryam when the Historian wasn't around, and she used her serious voice, so I understood this visit was a privilege and wished Gloria was there too.

Rani Aunty was tiny. I had never before seen a grown-up that small. She clutched me and cried, so I hugged her. She smelled of sandalwood soap and wore a long beaded skirt with a lace dupatta tucked into her waist and one end draped over her shoulder. Her skin was darker than mine. I remembered afterwards to tell Gloria that I was no longer the only *kallo* in the family, and my sister pinched my cheek and said I was the prettiest girl in the whole world. When she asked me what Rani looked like, I said, 'She's as pretty as me.'

The attic was a self-contained unit, despite its size. It suited its miniature occupant. The single room had been divided into a bedroom and sitting room. A bed, a table, a large steel trunk and a Singer sewing machine dominated the space. Beside the Singer sat a cardboard box overflowing with fabric and lace. A narrow bookshelf above the sewing machine held a few boxes, magazines and square biscuit tins. The floor was uneven and carpeted with worn rugs, layered over the bumps and dents. Two dusty louvred windows opened out to a view of the rest of our house and garden. I leaned out of one as far as I could and touched the tamarind tree, laughing when the Magician scolded and pulled me back. It would have made an ideal playroom. I imagined playing dress-ups here with Gloria and having tea afterwards with real cups and saucers, as Rani did. The framed Ganesh on the wall by the window appeared to be looking straight at me, questioning my acquisitiveness when my aunt had so little, and I was ashamed.

After that, Gloria and I took turns to go to the attic on alternate days with the Magician. Eventually the Magician allowed us both to come if we promised to behave. We leaned out of the window, marvelling at the sight of our house laid out in a neat grid below, and the trees we could touch if we stood on our tiptoes by the window.

'So Rani Aunty is a Hindu,' Gloria whispered one time by the window, pointing surreptitiously at the framed Ganesh and Baby Krishna on the wall. 'Her mum, our grandmother, must have been one. She must have been very religious. We don't have any holy pictures on our walls. I wonder...'

'Maybe that's why the Historian is so angry with her,' I said. 'Because she doesn't want to be a Person of the Book.' The word *kaffir* or unbeliever came to mind, but I couldn't bring myself to say it out loud because it was always used in anger in our house. Sometimes the aunties used the word to describe us, and if the Magician heard them she looked at them so sadly they made an extra effort to be nicer to us.

'Maybe, but at least the Magician doesn't seem to mind Rani Aunty being a *kaffir*.' Gloria lowered her voice further and I squeezed her hand, glad she'd thought it too.

When the Magician wasn't there, the aunties called Rani *pagli* or 'madwoman'. We had a few mad people in the family already, like the sleepwalking cousin and the old man who stood on his head every morning. One of the aunties muttered constantly, but no one called her mad, although the Historian said she was eccentric.

The aunties told us that Rani had been born normal but had become possessed when she was a teenager and it was best for everyone if she remained locked away. 'Just like that,' they said, snapping their fingers, 'she woke up one day and looked crazy. Cried for a week. Your father had to lock her up, poor little *pagli*.'

'It wasn't like that,' a tall woman, whose name we didn't know, interrupted. 'She didn't wake up crazy. She went away, remember? Or ran away with someone. Big scandal. Our Farah brought her back. That's when she lost her mind. Something must have happened then to make her *pagal*. We must ask Farah – she'll know.'

'She's not mad,' I said. 'Stop calling her a *pagli*. She's sweet and she doesn't shout or do anything scary. My father's the mad one.'

The aunties cackled and pinched my cheek, then shooed me away, ignoring us as they usually did. Gloria hugged me and said, 'Maybe she had a fit or something. You know how superstitious these old people are. No one can really be possessed. Anyway, we are not allowed to believe in *djinns* and all that. Let's see if Ammi knows.'

19

We went to find the Magician and she looked at us as if we had broken her heart – we knew that look. Her eyes shone and lines appeared near her mouth and she shook her head. She released her breath in a small sigh and went quiet for a minute. We counted under our breath. Then – 'Never say that again,' she said, 'never even think that. When you let people say bad things about your family, it makes you smaller. Always stand up for family. Would you believe people if they told you I was mad?'

'You're a *jadugar*,' we said together, and she smiled.

Four

Before Sohrab came to live with us, the Magician had been wary of boys in the house of women. Our brothers were allowed to have their friends in designated areas of the house. The garden room and bedrooms were off limits. But one of the aunties begged the Magician to let her teenage son live with a good family like ours.

'Farah, you don't know what mischief he gets up to in Bombay. His friends are wicked. He's a good boy and deserves a chance. Farah, we will die if you don't help. Here, in this healthy place with all this fresh air, he'll have that chance. Please let him come. I guarantee he will behave. After all, I am a mother of girls too,' the aunty wept and slapped her thighs with her hand.

'Sister, don't worry yourself. Of course you can ask the boy to come here if it would help.' The Magician was courteous as always, but her eyes darted quickly towards the secret room and she bit her lips.

The boy was called Habib, with thick hair that fell across his forehead and obscured his eyes. Within days of arriving at our house of health he was smoking with Warren, sneaking out at nights with both brothers, wearing their clothes and ignoring us completely. Gloria said it was like having another brother without being able to annoy him whenever we wanted to – no advantages for us, she said, only another smelly boy who ate too much and did too little. The Historian liked him, and our brothers were spared his fists on their faces for the months that Habib lived with us.

Habib's rehabilitation involved going to college with our brothers and playing badminton on the makeshift court Clive had rigged up outside. His mother was determined that he fill his lungs with as much good air as he could, before plunging him back into the evil smog and wicked distractions of Bombay.

'Living in Bombay means we are shortening our lives by five minutes every day,' Habib's mother said sorrowfully. 'So much pollution there, I can't even tell you. Not like here – clean and fresh. You children are lucky. You will live long and healthy lives.'

'Silly woman,' Gloria said in my ear. 'I wish she'd go away and take her useless son with her. I don't like him. He stares too much.'

'I haven't noticed.' I was surprised at Gloria's tone. 'I don't even know what colour his eyes are, all that hair in his face. You want me to accidently trip him up? Drop a spider on him when he sleeps?'

'You're such a criminal – no, you horrible creature, I don't want you to do anything to him.' Gloria flicked my cheek sharply but smiled and tossed her hair back. I watched Habib carefully over the next few days and found no evidence of staring. Then he was gone and we never saw him again. It was the Magician's way of easing Sohrab into the family – a sort of trial.

When Sohrab first came he was a curly-haired boy with thick spectacles and a funny accent. We came home from school one day and found him sitting in the kitchen with the Magician, sipping tea from a clear glass the Magician used only on special occasions, bunches of mint and cubes of sugar on a silver tray in front of him. 'Girls,' the Magician said in a high voice. 'Say hello to Sohrab. He is going to be your brother for a while. He will live with us. Maybe he can teach you to speak Farsi and you can teach him to speak English.'

'*Salaam,*' the boy said, turning pink when Gloria and I looked at him.

'*Salaam,*' we replied, giggling.

'Is his name really Sohrab, Ammi?' I asked. 'Like in that poem you read to us, "Sohrab and Rustum"?'

22

'Maryam, don't be rude. Yes, his name is Sohrab, and he is standing here, so you might want to talk to him directly.'

Sohrab removed his glasses in that nervous way that would become familiar to us, along with his shyness and inability to speak to Gloria without smoking a cigarette first. He polished the glasses with his head bent, and the Magician shot us a warning look. We composed our faces, walked up to her, kissed her and leaned against the bench, also with our heads lowered. The Magician straightened my hair and touched Gloria's cheek before kissing us back. We sniffed hungrily, threw our bags in the corner, slid the lid off the steel pot and helped ourselves to large serves of carrot halva, forgetting the boy on the chair who watched us.

'Are we living in a bloody *dharamshala*?' yelled the Historian that night after Sohrab left the table and we helped the Magician clear away the dishes. 'Did we need another of your strays in this house? Really? Did we? All these people coming and going. Where's that other boy, the nice one? This one doesn't speak. He doesn't look at us. Is he mute? What were you thinking? I suppose we'll have a whole family of refugees living here now.'

'He's not a refugee,' the Magician started to say as we crept out to find our brothers. 'And I will thank you not to —'

'Is Sohrab a refugee?' I asked my favourite brother Clive, who had to share a room with the new arrival, even though it was Warren who had the bigger room. Gloria said Warren was Daddy's pet and could do no wrong.

'I think he's just a student,' Clive said. 'He looks too good to be a refugee. Anyway, God knows what he's going to study, seeing as he can't speak English and no one here can speak Farsi.'

'The Magician speaks Farsi. Maybe she'll teach him.'

'Go away, Hannah. Go find someone else to annoy.'

After Sohrab came to live with us, the Magician started using strange Farsi words like *azizam* and *jun* as endearments, and cooking *fesenjoon* and chelo kebabs. I practised the words with Gloria when we were alone and worried that the Historian would find out about the Magician talking Farsi again. We remembered their fight. The Historian shouted that he was sick of her 'heathen language' and the Magician had said that shocking thing, so quietly that we thought we'd heard it wrong. But the look on the Historian's face told us he had heard it too.

'I will not allow a *rishwatkhor goonda* to tell me what I can and cannot say,' the Magician said in a voice like steel, and the Historian left the room. Every time after that, whenever the Historian yelled at my brothers and stormed through the house in his boots and police uniform, I would say '*rishwatkhor goonda*' in my head. The idea of my father being a corrupt thug made him less scary.

Now a new person jostled for the Magician's affection. Sohrab brought her black tea with mint every afternoon and hung around her as if she was *his* mother. She sighed and looked like someone we didn't recognise. She told us we had to be patient and love him like a brother because he missed his own brothers and sister. She brought out her copy of Matthew Arnold's 'Sohrab and Rustum' and read to me when I pestered her with questions:

> *I seek one man, one man, and one alone —*
> *Rustum, my father; who I hoped should greet,*
> *Should one day greet, upon some well-fought field,*
> *His not unworthy, not inglorious son.*

'Did he find his father?' I asked, even though I knew.
'Yes,' said the Magician, as if I didn't.
Poor Sohrab. He was terrified of Gloria and her silky laughing friends who tried to invite him to dance parties. He seemed permanently mortified. He sat with lowered eyes and swallowed rapidly at mealtimes, Adam's apple wobbling. I giggled uncontrollably the first time he sat with us, and Gloria kicked me under the

table and coughed to cover up my rudeness. He ate everything the Magician put in front of him, but rice made his tummy hurt. I heard him in the bathroom afterwards, moaning and gurgling. Sometimes he threw up. But he never told the Magician so she always gave him an extra helping of rice with every meal.

Such a misfit, our Sohrab. I was his only friend, although Clive was kind to him and tried to include him in everything we did. He wore tight shirts with stiff white collars and misshapen brown moccasins when other boys his age wore T-shirts and sneakers with laces. Gloria wondered why he didn't have any normal clothes like our brothers, and suggested we take him shopping. Mirabai, the day servant, was so offended by his shoes that she called him a dirty foreigner. 'Ganda firangi,' she muttered, whenever she saw him. 'Pagla kahin ka.' Dirty foreign madman from somewhere. She scowled, and the aunties shook their heads in agreement, whispering that this time Farah had gone too far. This boy was a total foreigner – not a hint of Indian in him. How on earth were they supposed to talk to him?

The Magician told us to talk to him in English, while she whispered in Farsi to him whenever the Historian wasn't there.

'But, Ammi,' Gloria said, 'we don't just speak English. We mix it up with Urdu and he gets confused. Anyway, he doesn't like me.'

'Darling.' The Magician pushed me to the side gently and held out her arm to Gloria. 'He's a shy boy, you know, shareef and decent. He's being respectful. Of course he likes you.'

'See, even the Magician mixes up languages,' I grinned up at her. 'I think our Sohrab will just have to get used to us. I can teach him some Urdu, if you like. Words like saala and bewakoof.'

'Maryam…' The Magician tried to look stern but her lips twitched and she laughed. She hardly laughed these days – she just…drooped. Her shoulders were round and soft and she looked so tired. She no longer wore her thick gold bangle because it kept sliding down over her wrist, interfering with her cooking. Under her baggy shalwar kameezes she was thin. Gloria said the fat aunties were to blame. They streamed in at mealtimes, and the Magician had no time to feed herself after they had all gone because it was time to start cooking the next meal.

That night, when we sat down to dinner, Meher Aunty shoved her bulk into the chair beside me. I turned and prodded her in the stomach and said, 'Such a big stomach you have!' Gloria sniggered and the Historian coughed loudly.

The Magician looked at me with shiny eyes and deep lines beside her mouth. I stood up when I heard her say, 'I am deeply sorry that my children are behaving like urchins. I have failed in my duty as a mother and most humbly ask your pardon. Hannah, go to your room. You too, Gloria. Stay there until you become better human beings.'

Outside the dining room door, Gloria wiped my tears and whispered, 'She had to say that. She doesn't think we're urchins. We'll go back together and say sorry later. Really, Hannah, that was funny, but don't do it again. We can't make the Magician sad, okay?'

The Magician made sure I didn't sit next to Meher Aunty at mealtimes again, just in case.

Five

'Gloria, why do you think the Historian keeps Rani Aunty locked up? She doesn't seem mad or bad.' We sat on the lower branches of the stunted mango tree in the garden and Gloria plaited my hair. A dry, flaky breeze picked up leaves and swirled them around in circles near our feet. It was a warm Sunday afternoon and the house was quiet except for the snoring aunties and the click-clack of the Magician's knitting. The Historian was in the library and had shooed us away when we looked in at the window.

'He's madder and badder,' she said, tugging gently to get the knots out of my hair.

'He is, isn't he? He's definitely the mad one. And she's his only sister, which makes it worse.' I giggled, but looked around for the object of our conversation to materialise, as he often did.

'Half-sister. They had different mothers. Old Grandpa Billy was a lady's man and had lots of ladies trailing after him, but you, sweet Hannah, are one twisted little monster.' Gloria finished braiding and tied my hair at the ends with two lengths of red ribbon, the ends of which she had knotted and threaded with beads.

'Thanks,' I said, and she swung my plaited hair at my cheek, making it sting a little.

I jumped from the tree and she followed, screwing up her face when she scraped her knee. We heard voices and checked each other quickly — no missing buttons, dresses not too grubby, hair tied up. We brushed leaves and twigs off one another and tried to look as if we had been standing by the tree. The Historian had rules. Girls did not climb trees.

The Historian appeared around the corner, followed by my brothers and Sohrab. They carried spades and shovels and wore miserable faces. Warren, in a new shirt, looked as if he'd been nabbed on his way to meet Joyce, his girlfriend.

'Start digging, boys,' the Historian said, pointing to a neglected part of the garden he had always intended for his roses. The gardener had already begun to loosen some of the dirt.

Clive picked up a shovel and started digging without a word. He too had learned early not to stand up to the Historian. Warren folded his arms across his chest.

The Historian frowned. 'Well, Your Highness? Are you waiting for a written invitation? Or is there something wrong with your hearing?'

'C'mon, Dad, you don't think we are going to dig holes all day, do you?' Warren flicked a speck of dust off his arm and smoothed back his hair. The Historian clenched his fist. I slipped behind Gloria. Any minute now the Historian's hand would connect with Warren's cheek. Sohrab picked up two shovels, thrust one at Warren and placed himself between them.

Gloria tugged at the Historian's arm. 'What sort of roses will we have here? Can we have climbing ones as well?'

The Historian called out to the gardener and unclenched his fist. Warren and Sohrab started digging alongside Clive, and I winked at Sohrab when he turned his head towards me. Gloria stepped back. With a hand over her mouth, she said this was where the Historian would hide the bodies, then saw the terror on my face and hugged me. 'I'm just being silly. Don't look so scared. Let's go and see if the mangoes are ripe.'

The boys dug while Mali Baba, the gardener, an old Nepali man who spoke limited Hindi, sprinkled manure and water in the patch of dirt they turned over. Gloria and I watched from under the mango tree. The Historian stood around for a while, crisply giving orders, warning our brothers not to slack off, then turned on his heel and walked away. When he didn't come back, we climbed back into the tree and looked for mangoes. The boys laughed and threw handfuls of dirt at each other, their voices drifting up to us, and we chucked green mangoes at them. Warren complained about his shirt and how Joyce would break up with him, and Sohrab took off his glasses and handed them to me. Then they put down their spades and held their arms out, catching us as we jumped down with muffled squeals. Mali Baba pottered around, raking, forking, turning.

The next morning I waited by the pond for the gardener to come and fetch water with his tin cans. I followed him and asked him about the classic roses the Historian had wanted for so long. He was irritable when I hung around. He planted six bare sticks in that circular patch of earth my brothers had dug out. I watched the stalks every day for two weeks, waiting for them to sprout and look more rose-like, but nothing happened and I gave up, nearly forgetting about them until Mali Baba beckoned me one morning and led me to the patch. The stalks were now tall bushes with elegant fingers extending upwards, covered with red–green leaves and tiny buds. I ran to the library and asked the Historian to come outside with me.

'What for?' he asked, eyebrows coming together in that familiar what-have-you-done-now way.

'Just come, please. It's a surprise. Come.'

We stood and looked at the upright bushes with their buds poised to open and he smiled.

'Are they classic roses? English roses?' he asked.

'Yes, they are. And they're all pink.'

They thrived in the Historian's body patch, those roses, despite being neither classic nor English, nor even pink. They survived the heat and cold and the monsoons that washed away the Magician's hyacinths every year. Sometimes I like to think they are still there, blooming, despite demolitions and departures.

Six

On the day the Magician decided that Sohrab would have his own room, the Historian was listening to BBC radio. We had heard the scratchy voice of a foreign woman talking about Americans when we'd passed by the library earlier. I missed being in the library in the afternoons. The Historian was home a lot these days and I couldn't be with my conquistadors. He didn't let us listen to music any more, so we hung around and annoyed the Magician and our brothers instead. We made a lot of noise, Gloria and I, as we shouted and bumped against each other while pretending to help move Sohrab's things out of Clive's room.

'It's really not fair, Ammi,' Gloria complained. 'The boys always get what they want. Why can't I have a room of my own? You know what Hannah's like. She screams and snores. You try sleeping with her and see for yourself.'

'*Bache log*, my sweet children,' said the Magician, kissing us absently. 'You know it's an important year for Clive and Sohrab. They both need the space to study. When you go to college, you'll get a room of your own. Now, help me carry this chair – good – now put it down there.'

The radio went silent and we looked at each other. The Magician held a finger to her lips as the Historian erupted into the room. Gloria clamped her hand on my arm and we tried to edge out. The Magician put on her patient face and crossed her arms loosely.

'Where is he? Where's Sohrab?' The Historian looked around the room.

'What's happened?'

'The revolution, that's what! Those bloody fool *mullahs* have taken over the country. Oh, for God's sake, don't any of you know what's going on in the world? I'm talking about Iran – yes, your wonderful Iran. I think we're stuck with our little refugee indefinitely. He can't go back to his bloody country now. They're killing everyone. Thrown out the Shah and declared the place an Islamic Republic. Bloody thugs. And some of the jokers have taken over the American Embassy in Tehran. As if the Americans are going to sit and do nothing about that. Mark my words, bloodbath to follow. Too many idiots running these countries – where's a good dictator when you need one?'

Sohrab stood by the pond, smoking quickly and tossing the stubs into the water. I felt sorry for the turtles that moved slowly through its purple haze, and hoped they wouldn't swallow any. Gloria patted his arm and didn't turn her face away from the smoke he blew at her.

'I must go, *khanum*,' Sohrab said, taking off his glasses and wiping his eyes. 'I must go back before they close the borders. Before the Shah takes his revenge. I must find Baba and Maman *jun*. The Shah was a bastard but the *mullahs* are worse.'

'Can't you ring them first?' Gloria was the practical sort. 'See how they are? They might be all right and you won't need to worry about them. Maybe go a little later, when things have settled down? It's dangerous to go when it's so chaotic. I'm sure your parents will be safe. Don't worry.'

Sohrab slumped his shoulders and gripped the back of his neck with his hand, but said nothing.

'Are you a refugee now?' I asked, and Gloria pinched my arm.

Sohrab continued to puff and cough. 'We are all refugees now, Maryam *azizam*.'

'You can live with us forever, you know that.'

'Thank you.' Sohrab chucked the last cigarette butt into the pond and bowed slightly in our direction. One of the turtles turned over. I reached in and turned him around, watching as he paddled away. He didn't look right. There were lots of turtles here once. Now we had two and I had promised to look after them. The pond was full of cigarette stubs but I couldn't chide Sohrab, not now, when he had just become a refugee.

'My brother Reza is involved with the Americans in the embassy,' Sohrab said in his scratchy cigarette voice. He stared at the pond. 'Reza will make trouble for my family. For Baba and Maman *jun*. Now they have to live with this shame. Reza listens to his friend Mahmud, and Mahmud is very dangerous. Like Amrika. Both dangerous. But Amrika is the real *shaitoon*. My country is screwed. My Baba spent his lifetime burning his eyes in oil furnaces for the benefit of bastard Amrika – now this. The ayatollahs are useless. Religion is useless. We are all going to die, *khanum*.'

We put our arms around him then, because we didn't know what else we could do. He smelled of smoke and sweat, and his face was damp and pink. But at least he was talking to Gloria now. And she was happy about that; her left cheek dimpled quickly before she put on her serious, concerned face. Sohrab took off his large glasses and looked blindly into the distance.

We didn't want to die and we didn't want him to die. The Magician would figure out a way to keep us all alive.

Seven

On the wall of his room, Sohrab tacked a map of Iran and circled towns with a red ballpoint. Abadan. Ahvaz. Khorramshahr. Isfahan. Tabriz. Shiraz. Tehran. He stared at this map for hours and wrote in curly Farsi script on the margins. His glasses were streaked and cloudy and he didn't care. His English was getting worse and the Magician had to speak to his lecturers at the college and request an extension on his assignments. The aunties said he was traumatised and needed to be among his own people. The Historian said that for once he agreed with them. It was time Sohrab went back – after all, he couldn't stay with us forever and if he wasn't studying what was he doing?

'Oh, I'm sick of those old women and their endless advice. Maybe they can go back to their own people instead of filling your ears with their nonsense.' The Magician put her sketchbook down with a thump when we repeated what we'd heard. We stared and she rearranged her face, although the shiny eyes and deep lines near her mouth worried us. She'd gone back to wearing her well-ironed shalwar kameez suits, with their long wraparound dupattas instead of scrunched-up pyjama pants and old shirts. Her wrists were still bare, though, and I missed the chunky gold bangle. Her skin was too soft and her voice too sharp these days.

'Hannah told them we are his people,' Gloria's arm circled mine.

'And that's the truth, my Maryam.' The Magician smiled briefly and the lines disappeared. 'I hope you weren't rude.'

'She didn't punch Meher Aunty in the tummy, if that's what you mean.'

The Magician shook her head at us, wagging a finger and holding out her arms as we rushed at her, breathing her in, fighting to get closer. She asked about school, checked our heads for nits and reached behind her for a bag of almonds and gave us some. This was Sohrab's fault – the almonds instead of sweets – because ever since Sohrab had come to live with us, the Magician had remembered she was half-Persian. And Persians ate nuts and drank black tea with mint. The sticky toffees that were our weekly treats had been replaced by daily handfuls of almonds and pistachios, bland and tasteless. I filled my pockets with them and hid them inside the wardrobe because food must never be thrown away. I would need to do something about that soon. Gloria had shouted when she saw the line of ants crawling beneath her clothes.

'Go and find Sohrab and tell him I want my tea, Maryam *jun*. Gloria, you stay here. I need you to try this,' the Magician said, holding up the red cardigan she was knitting, which I would inherit after Gloria finished school this year.

Sohrab was already in the kitchen, arranging biscuits on a plate beside two pale glasses of tea. He turned around with a vague smile when I clapped my hands and said, 'Sohrab, you're a good *chaiwala*. Come on, the Magician wants her tea – she's in your room. I can carry that.' I picked up the tray and he followed me out.

Back in the room, the Magician held a cardigan against Gloria and asked, 'Did your arms suddenly grow longer? I'll need to add more rows. That means more wool. I hope I can get the same again. Next year you girls can knit your own cardigans. I'll show you. Time you learned something useful.'

'Gloria's a freak,' I said to Sohrab. 'She has very long arms.'

Sohrab didn't smile. He put the tray down beside the Magician and added two lumps of sugar to her tea, then sat down with his steaming glass and stared into the distance. The tea cooled between them and Gloria picked up the red cardigan with its sleeves still unfinished and winked at me. The Magician spoke gently in Farsi, and I tried not to mind. I didn't like these moments she spent with Sohrab, cocooned away from the rest of us, speaking a secret language only he understood. I settled into the curve of her arm, breathing in her minted tea, listening to the gurgle of her throat as she sipped. She was lovely, my Magician – so good, so warm, so constant.

Eight

The Magician worried that Rani Aunty's attic was crumbling down around her. A new layer of white dust had settled on everything. Whenever we went to Rani's room, we wiped the chairs, the shelves, the table and the railings on the iron bed.

One day, a week after Sohrab's revolution, we found Rani standing on a chair, trying to wipe the shelf above her sewing machine. The Magician rushed forward and helped her down, scolding and laughing at the same time.

'Are you trying to kill yourself, Rani? This is why I bring the girls with me. If you need something done, let the young ones do it.'

'I'm just trying to wipe the shelf. I think I know where this white dust is coming from.' She pointed at the shelf she'd been wiping, folding her arms and peering upwards. 'See? It's the ants. So much wood here, plenty for them to eat. Nothing we can do.'

'Oh, yes, we can,' the Magician said firmly. 'I'll get some lime to cover up the holes. That should get rid of them.'

'Nothing but acid gets rid of them,' said Rani, 'and I'm not going to let you bring acid into this room.'

The Magician and Rani Aunty tried to stare each other down while I pulled out fabric from the box that always sat beside the Singer, and folded soft swathes of georgette and silk, laying them on top of the coarser cotton and *khadi*. The silks were hard to fold, with a bouncy, slippery texture that resisted neat squares, so I gave up and bundled them back in the box, draping them artistically over the sides. The Magician and Rani sat down with cups of tea and watched me trawl through the box.

'Careful, Maryam,' the Magician said, as she always did, for I was prone to little disasters, spillages, tears.

'Let her be,' Rani said, also as she always did, smiling down at me.

'Here,' I said, jumping up from the floor and on to the chair beside the fabric box. 'I'll clean your shelves properly, Rani Aunty.'

'Careful.' This time they both spoke and held out their hands towards me.

I brought down all the boxes, books, magazines and tins from the long narrow shelf, passing them down to the Magician and Rani, slowly wiping each section of the shelf, noticing how it creaked if I put pressure on it. At the corners there were little holes, where the wood had been completely eaten away. I thought guiltily about the nuts I was hiding in the cupboard and wondered if the ants eating Rani's shelves were the ones I had fostered.

'I don't think you should put any of the heavy boxes back,' I said to Rani when I'd finished. 'It looks like it's about to fall down. Why can't we put another shelf up instead?'

'What a good idea!' The Magician clapped the heel of her palm against her forehead. 'Yes, that's what we'll do. I'll get the carpenter to come and take this away and make you another one.'

'Where am I going to put all this?' Rani pointed at the boxes that blocked her path to the sewing machine. We looked. There was hardly any room between the Singer and the little table where she ate her meals.

'Maryam will help you sort it out. I have to go, but I'll be back in an hour.' And the Magician went out quickly, locking the door, leaving me alone for the first time with my aunt.

I opened tins and boxes, flipped through magazines, tried on unfinished skirts and forgot that I was supposed to be helping Rani sort her belongings into categories to be labelled and stored. She watched me closely and stroked my arm the way the Magician did and asked, 'Are you missing something, Maryam?'

I patted myself down, looked for missing buttons, or worse, undone buttons, and finding everything in order, replied, 'I haven't lost anything today, Rani Aunty. Why? Have you found something of mine?'

She opened her mouth but closed it again quickly, instead picking up a slim tin box with a picture of Little Bo Peep on its lid. She looked around nervously. 'I want you to keep this safe but you must never open it. It's very important. Remember, keep it somewhere safe. Hide it so no one finds it, but do not look inside. Can you do that for me, Maryam? Can you promise?' Without looking at me or waiting for a response, she wrapped the tin in brown paper, tied it with a piece of lace from her fabric box and tucked the box under my arm. Then she pulled out a dense green dupatta from the same box and wrapped it around me, hiding the tin completely. Her urgency was contagious and I didn't object, nodding when she tilted my chin to look into my eyes, caressing my cheek with her fingers. The tin was weightless and its shape dug into my underarms.

When the Magician returned with Gloria she brought two large cardboard boxes to store Rani's things downstairs if needed. Rani pulled out a large square of silk and offered it to Gloria saying, 'Maryam chose the green one and said you would like this one.'

I wondered if Rani's tongue would turn black at the lie she had just told. I could keep a secret but I wasn't allowed to lie. Lies make our tongues go black and put black spots on our souls. We knew that from Sunday school with Sister Angelina.

Nine

Three new hardcover books had appeared in the library, and it looked like someone wanted to keep them hidden. Unlike the conquistador books and Grandfather's diaries, these were green. Gloria no longer bothered with the library. She clattered around the house in high heels, laughing with her silly friends, hiding things from me and grumbling when I asked her to plait my hair. She used to love doing that. Now she tossed her nose in the air when I asked her something and said she didn't want to play silly baby games with me any more. Once, I saw her wince sharply when pulling her jeans up over her bum, and I wondered if she hurt down *there*, where the aunties told us we would hurt when we grew up because we were girls. The Magician said Gloria was growing up and I said I preferred it if she didn't.

I spent afternoons in the library on my own, when the Historian was away. I memorised the order in which the books were laid out, shuffled them around to test myself and put them back as I found them. I knew the exact moment the new books arrived because I was hiding behind the Historian's desk when the door opened. I shut my eyes and stayed still. Footsteps padded around the room; the stepladder was lifted and placed by the bookshelves; the cushion squeaked slightly as someone stood on it; then all the sounds were reversed and the room was quiet again. I stayed in my curled-up position for a little while longer before creeping out to look for Gloria.

'So, what's all the fuss about?' Gloria looked around and shrugged my hand off. 'This had better not be a scheme to make me read the diaries, Hannah.'

'No, honest, I heard someone come in and do something, put something somewhere. Just stay here till I find it. Please?'

'Holy Mary, Mother of God, save your heathen soul and grant me patience.'

'You sound like Sister Angelina,' I said, scanning the shelves, looking for clues that would reveal the mystery. 'You shouldn't make fun of the sisters. They're married to God. That's how they talk.'

Gloria stuck her tongue out and folded her arms across her chest.

'I found them.'

Gloria reached up and I passed three green hardcover journals down to her and climbed off the stepladder. We ran to the spot behind the Historian's desk, sat down and stared at each other. I kept an eye on the door as we opened the first one, then the other two. Gloria didn't read anything out loud and I didn't ask her to.

'Put them back,' Gloria whispered after a while. 'Exactly where you found them.'

I watched those books. No one took them away or added to them. The aunties and I wiped the books every week and I cleaned the shelf that held the hidden journals. I guarded them for the next two years, briefly looking inside, puzzling, wondering.

Ten

Something made the Historian pace outside our room at night, and my dreams became less terrifying than the fact that he was there, outside my door. Gloria slept with me and stroked my hair until I fell asleep, and sometimes she was still in my bed in the mornings. The Magician had whispered conversations with him but the pacing continued. When she came in to check on us, we kept our eyes closed and didn't move. The Historian never came in. The sound of his shiny police boots click-clacking in the passage filled my head so completely that I heard them everywhere: at school, in the Magician's kitchen, on the grass. He walked up and down outside our room every night, and Gloria said she couldn't decide whom she would like to kill first, him or me.

One night, one of the aunties bumped into him on her way to the toilet and screamed.

'Calm down, woman, it's me, Gordon. Stop this noise at once!'

'Godden? Godden? What are you doing here? Why are you still all dressed up? Scaring poor old women to death! Is Farah all right? Something wrong with the girls?'

'No, nothing's wrong. Stop shouting, you'll wake the whole house. And why are you still here? Weren't you supposed to go back to your son's house yesterday?'

'Oh Godden, so now you're asking me to leave in the middle of the night? *Hai hai*, my son told me this would happen. Farah, Farah, I cannot stay in this house for one more minute.'

The Magician ran down the passageway and doors opened, spilling out brothers and cousins and Sohrab. Gloria uncurled her body from around me and said, 'We may as well stop pretending to sleep. The entire *tamasha* is happening just outside our door.' We rolled off my bed and joined the chaos.

Such a sight we were. Gloria in her pretty lace nightie and me in a long T-shirt that had belonged to one of my brothers. Warren and Clive and Sohrab, bare-chested and sleepy. The aunties and the Magician in their cotton nightgowns and the Historian looking irritated in formal police gear, three silver stars on his shoulder strap, crossed sword and baton. 'Go away, all of you,' he said with a growl in his voice. 'Go back to sleep and stop this *tamasha*. A man cannot walk in his own home? I live in a zoo and the monkeys are hungry. Is that it? Shall I throw you a banana? What's wrong with all of you? See, now the children are awake. They'll be too tired to go to school in the morning and whose fault is that? Boys, get out of my sight, you insolent thugs, wandering around naked in a house full of women – girls, back to bed. Now.'

'That's our entertainment for tonight,' Gloria yawned and climbed back into her own bed when the crowd outside our door disappeared. 'If the dream bothers you again, Hannah, think of all the fun we've just had. Who needs a circus when you live here? Maybe we get to skip school if we are tired tomorrow.'

'I don't think so,' the Magician said in the morning, ignoring our open-mouthed yawns and whining. 'When I was a little girl I had to get up at four am and clean the fireplace before my wicked stepmother got up, then make breakfast for my wicked stepsisters, then go to school and get top marks, *then* — '

We laughed and she straightened our school uniforms, kissed us and pointed at the steel glasses of warm milk that waited for us on the benchtop.

∞

After four days, the Historian stopped his pacing and the dreams stopped too. I missed Gloria's body in my bed and faked a nightmare; but, like the Magician, she knew when I lied and threatened to slap me if I tried that again.

The aunties twitched their dupattas and turned their faces away whenever they saw the Historian. He had broken the golden rule of hospitality. He had asked a visitor, a guest in our house, to leave. Despite the Magician's tears and apologies, all the aunties, except fat Aunt Meher, packed their bags and left in the next few days.

'We are not beggars, Farah,' they said. 'We know when we are not welcome in your house. This is the price you pay when you marry someone from outside. You can't expect a foreigner to understand our ways. Now you'll just have to bring up all these mixed-breed children on your own.'

'Stupid old women,' muttered Gloria as we watched them pack their bags and bundles and grumble at the Magician. 'They should be kissing the floor our mother walks on. Good riddance, I say. I hope they never come back. And I hope that horrible cockroach Meher also goes. But she won't. We'll all die before she leaves us alone.'

'Good riddance,' I echoed, shocked at Gloria's words, her low grumbles, her venom. Distracted by the thought that I could now take charge of the books in the library, I squeezed Gloria's hand and looked towards the Historian. He had sent the aunties away. No more old women with dusters and gossip. All those books, blue and gold and three green ones – all mine at last. I would find out what Gloria saw in the books. I would know what made her catch her breath and become shiny-eyed.

The Historian had made this possible. I went to stand beside him and clasped his arm, stroking it, trying to smile. He frowned down at me, his pale blue eyes calm under thick brows, and swung me off the ground. He smelled of Old Spice and his hands were warm. The last time he had carried me was when I was four. Then the nightmares started and I wouldn't let him touch me. I wriggled and he set me back down, keeping his arm around my shoulders. 'Are you menstruating, Hannah? You're old enough, aren't you? You smell a bit —' he said, and I shivered.

Eleven

The Magician was distracted. She seemed to miss the aunties, even though she had been impatient with them lately. Meher Aunty was the only one who still clumped around, sat down first for every meal and made me want to punch her stomach. Gloria and I scowled at her and she stared back with unblinking round eyes, forcing us to break contact first.

In Sohrab's room, the Magician sat with her sketchbook open on her lap and stared into the distance. When I put my arms around her and asked why she was sad, she smiled and said, 'I'm thinking.'

'About what?'

'Nothing important.' The Magician tapped her pencil on the book and patted my arm. Her hands were dry and lined, as if she was no longer using the Lacto Calamine she used for everything, even our chicken pox scabs. She had stopped going to the Sunday markets, instead sending Gloria and me with lists and instructions.

I thought about the sketches in the green hardcover books. I knew they were hers. They had to be. The flowers threw me at first — dozens of sketches of flowers — because the Magician had never shown an interest in flowers, preferring to sketch us as we grew and changed. We didn't always like what she claimed she saw in our faces, but Gloria said artists were allowed to be mysterious. I found sketches of people too, in those green books, and writing — the same curly Farsi script with which Sohrab covered his map.

A woman wearing a sari reminded me of the Magician. But why would my mother do a self-portrait? And what of that shadow sketch of a mother and child – with their faces blank and arms akimbo? And why was she writing in Farsi? What was it she didn't want anyone to read?

'What is it, Maryam? Why is it so hard for you to sit still? Do you have worms in your stomach? Ants in your pants?'

Before I could reply, Sohrab shuffled in and looked at us blankly, as if he'd forgotten who we were. The Magician clicked her tongue and asked him to go and make tea. 'And Maryam, go and find Gloria. I have something important to say to you both.'

When I returned with Gloria, the Magician said, 'Okay, girls, I can't have Sohrab brooding any more. We must do something.'

'Buy him some new clothes,' Gloria said. 'That should cheer him up. Works for me every time.'

'And I get all your old ones.' I dug my elbow into Gloria's tummy.

'First, we need to purify his surroundings.'

The Magician outlined her plan. Sohrab's heart was sick and needed healing. It was more than two years since the revolution and he was still grieving. We needed to drive the *djinns* away. We needed to bring peace back to the house. She listed what we would need: incense, oil, small earthenware bowls, rice, sugar, yoghurt, honey, fennel seeds, brahmi, a silver coin, the Qur'an and the red-bearded *maulvi* who lived in the house beside the mosque.

Gloria and I helped to carry things from the kitchen to Sohrab's room. We were allowed to put flowers in a vase and decorate the small lamp table with paper doilies and incense sticks. The *maulvi* chanted prayers in Arabic. After he'd finished, he took out a piece of paper from his pocket, folded it into a tiny square and gave it to the Magician. She placed it inside a small brown pouch, sewed it tightly, and looped a length of black string around it. Sohrab sat on a chair with his head on his chest and didn't speak.

'Here, Sohrab, take this, my son. This *taveez* will keep you from all harm.' The Magician's voice was gentle but Sohrab shivered and looked away.

46

'*Jadu-tona*,' whispered Gloria. 'We're not allowed to believe in spirits and things, but this is good magic and Sohrab will get better. He's got to believe in it or it won't work.'

'*Merci, khanum*,' Sohrab mumbled, 'but I must go back to Iran. That is what I must do. My country is burning and the ayatollahs have locked up everyone who doesn't agree with them. I must be with Baba and Maman *jun*. I must find my brothers. Prayers cannot help me.'

'Of course, if that's what you want. We will help you.' The Magician sounded tired.

We thanked the *maulvi*, and the Magician placed an envelope in his hand. He bowed and left, blessing us all. He used to come to our house once a week when we were younger. We chanted sections of the Qur'an with him, following his finger as it moved across the page. We couldn't read Arabic, having learned by rote everything we were supposed to, and he knew that. He was an old man now, bent and scrawny, and only came on special occasions.

The Magician said we should light incense for forty days at twilight because there were many burdens on us and it wouldn't hurt to purify us all. We did this secretly, because we all knew what the Historian thought of the Magician's rituals and practices. Sohrab started coming to the table at mealtimes instead of shuffling through the house like a sleepwalker. He was angry now – 'Bloody *mullahs*,' he muttered, 'bloody Americans, bloody Indians keeping me in this bloody village' – and the Magician said that was a sign he was waking up.

We lit incense and burned fennel seeds and placed a drop of honey on our tongues every evening. We mixed yoghurt with jaggery and ate a teaspoon of the mixture before prayers. We listened to prayers in Arabic and Farsi in Sohrab's room for forty days. And on the forty-first day, the Magician disappeared.

Part II

Immigrants

No one knows about the beetles in the grass at dawn because no one ever sees them. Red velvet beetles that close up in a dot of scarlet when I touch them.

No one ever sees white pyjama-clad ghosts come to the bed and reach under the mosquito netting.

No one sees the Magician tiptoe across the house and push open the door into the midnight garden, and no one hears her come back just after dawn.

No one notices the silence in Sohrab's room; no one sees the child silhouetted in a flash of light by the library window; no one stops the muscular arm holding the brick that crashes through the window.

No one.

Twelve

The peacock is the national bird of India and the lotus its national flower. Both bird and flower are fussy, rare creatures, to be admired and sighed over when spotted. Peacock feathers are considered unlucky. Even so, the Magician had a peacock feather duster she used to flick over her crystal, and she was the most superstitious of women. She believed she avoided bad luck by hanging the duster on a rusty nail outside the kitchen door, but the urchin children who hung around the neighbourhood used to pinch the feathers. That made her tighten her mouth and mumble something in Farsi under her breath.

I did not expect to see large peacocks strolling about in the corridors of my university in Perth or hear them calling out in the courtyard in the middle of a lecture. They cried out like demented cats and flew over balustrades and perched on balconies, arching their backs grandly when they had an audience. Most Australian students ignored them, while the rest of us stopped and took photos.

A tall, dark-haired girl with deeply dimpled cheeks stood beside me one morning as I watched the birds. She wore tight jeans and an emerald silk top that slid off her shoulder to expose a purple bra strap. She dropped into place beside me as we queued to get inside the lecture hall and grinned. I smiled back and sat with her, noticing she didn't take notes or show any interest in Australian children's literature. She seemed to wake up at the end of the hour and spoke for the first time as we stepped outside, looking at the peacocks again.

'Hi, I'm Anya. I hate these birds, but you seem fascinated. Don't you have lots of them in your country?' She sounded like a melodious version of Chekov from *Star Trek*.

'Yes, but they don't walk around in buildings like they do here. We had to go to a zoo to look at one. I'm Hannah, by the way.'

'I know,' she said and I wondered how.

'Why do you hate the peacocks?' I asked instead.

'What's to like? Noisy, showy creatures, strutting about as if they own the place. They do help to keep me awake during lectures, so I suppose I shouldn't complain.'

We walked across the green stretch of lawn towards the river as she talked, her hand tucked surprisingly into the curve of my arm. It was a hot morning, the river so blue and the heat so expansive I was disoriented. In my childhood, heat was always contained by rain. Perth's long dry summers bleached the trees and silenced the birds. Long strips of bark lay extravagantly on the path, and the sting of sun on my neck made me wince. Anya wrapped a long scarf around her shoulders and said, 'Hotter than hell, don't you think?' We crossed Hackett Drive and stopped beside her car, a green Daihatsu with plastic animals nodding on the dash. Her bracelets jangled as she got in, wound down the window and said, 'See you tomorrow, then. You've got history at eleven, don't you? Me too. We'll have lunch after, okay?' My first week at university and I had a friend.

Anya offered me a lift home the next day. I accepted, glad not to have to wait for the bus and knowing the Historian would still be at work. She drove fast, braked abruptly, swerved around corners, and her music flared over our shouted conversation.

'It's a long way from here,' I yelled. 'Are you sure you want to take me home? You can drop me off in the city and I can take a bus.'

'No problems. I like driving.'

Outside the stone and timber house I shared with the Historian and my brothers, she skidded to a stop, whistled and said,

'Nice – you should see the dump I live in.' She followed me to the kitchen and walked straight to the fridge, poured herself an orange juice and threw her bag on the tiled floor. 'Got anything to eat? I'm starving.'

I looked inside the fridge. 'A sandwich?'

'Great. Got any ham?'

'No, sorry. We don't eat ham. What about chicken?' I made sandwiches and she ate hers rapidly, helped herself to more orange juice and asked if it was okay to smoke inside. She laughed at the look on my face and walked out through the kitchen door – whistling again at the sight of the Swan Valley stretched out before us. It was pretty: green despite the crumbling heat; vineyards meeting sheep at the edge of wire fences; tractors in the distance; white alpacas scattering at the sound of cars on the highway. The smell of honey drifted in on a slow breeze, reminding me of Gloria, her hair and skin. Dave the beekeeper must be up and about. Nothing kept him from checking his hives twice a day. And there he was, bobbing up behind the fence in his veil. He lifted a hand and I waved back.

The Historian's garden was a mystery to him. He had no idea how things grew and what to do when they grew too high. He tried to get my brothers interested but they resisted, taller than him now and unthreatened by the size of his fists. So we had Greg instead. Greg kept the garden beds mulched and the lawns mown. He charged fifteen dollars an hour and didn't take the rubbish away. He spread it under the jacaranda and coral tree and stunted wattles, and said it would eventually break down. All it did was blow around in the wind. It was my job to collect the grass clippings and weeds and tree prunings in plastic bags and throw them in the council bin every week. The Historian grumbled about how crowded the bin was and I said he should pay Greg to take the rubbish away.

'Want one?' Anya asked, holding out a packet of Winfield Blue, and I shook my head. 'Your dad must be doing all right – places like these don't come cheap. Holy shit. Is that a Jag in the carport?'

'Don't get too excited. It doesn't go anywhere. It's a dud he bought to impress his clients. He's like that.'

Anya laughed and blew smoke through her nostrils. 'What does your old man do to make this kind of dough? Mine's a rotten old bastard and I can't wait to leave home. Where's your mum? Does she work too?'

'I haven't got a mum. I mean – I do, but she's not here. I don't know where she is. She walked out on us. And my dad's a rotten old bastard too.'

She reached across and linked arms with me and threw away the smouldering cigarette. 'Gotta go. You're sweet. Thanks for lunch. Next time I'll take you to my place.' I squished the cigarette into the ground and picked up the dead stub before following her in.

Anya invited me to her house one morning when neither of us could summon the energy to wait for our next class. The sun was a powerful deterrent against stretching out on the grass outside the library as we normally did. Groups of students walked quickly across the oval to sit on benches under the trees as we decided to wag classes for the rest of the day.

'You may as well meet my crazy parents,' she said, squinting against the glare of a ferocious March sun, scrabbling in her shoulder bag for sunglasses and keys. 'My place is a friggin' dump, so don't get your hopes up.' She unlocked the car and said, 'Of course we could die of heat stroke before we ever get to my place.' We squealed when our legs touched the vinyl seats, and Anya snatched up a beach towel to place on the driver's seat. I wound the windows down and gasped in the boxed heat.

Anya's house was one of three on a brand-new street in a suburb I'd never heard of, to the north of the city. Bundles of bricks and steel frames lay on each side of the road. She screeched to a stop outside a beige-brick house with an upward-curving driveway and piles of yellow sand and concrete mixers on the verge. A koala letterbox was plonked in the middle of the sand with the number 22 dangling from its arms. 'Home sweet home,' Anya said. 'It's a construction site. My parents don't know how to live in a proper home. They're from Estonia and people don't have houses there – only buildings and factories.'

At the front door we heard an electric drill and a loud clatter. A bearded man in a singlet and jeans turned as we entered, a cigarette clenched between his teeth. Several planks of wood lay near his feet and the drill was still going in his right hand.

'My dad's building a catamaran.' Anya's voice was low. 'He's a friggin' arsehole and my mum's useless. Doesn't want to learn English or get a job.' A woman in a pink dressing gown waved her cigarette in our direction from behind the kitchen counter.

Anya said loudly, 'Mum, Dad – we have a visitor.'

The woman raised an eyebrow and put down a magazine she was holding. 'You want coffee?'

'Yes,' Anya said sharply. 'We'll have coffee. What else you got?'

'*Pierogi*?'

'Always friggin' *pierogi*? Why can't you make sandwiches like other mums?'

'Anya.' The bearded man spoke, and the violence in his voice reminded me of the Historian. 'You no speak to your mother like that – you want sandwich, you make sandwich. You big girl now and you got hands – use them.' He smiled at me and continued, 'Hello, friend of Anya. Sit. I will bring you coffee.'

'Yes, sit. What is your name? You from another country too – like us, yeah?' Anya's mother walked over and placed her hand on my arm. She smelled of smoke and dishwashing liquid. Her hair was pale yellow and twisted on top of her head with a butter-fly clip.

'Yes. I'm Hannah. From India.'

'Hannah. You good girl. You make my Anya good. She no have many friends. She look like tough, but inside she like butter.' She waved the smoke from her dying cigarette away from my face and hugged me, her arms crackling static as she pulled the dressing gown tighter around her waist.

Anya lifted her face to the ceiling and snorted.

∞

'They like you,' Anya said afterwards, driving me home. 'That makes a change. Still, be different if you were a boy. They were very rude to the boys I brought home.'

'I would never take a boy home,' I said. 'The Historian – my father, that is – would lock me up forever, like he locked up his poor mad sister.'

'So what's the story with your mum? What mad sister? What happened?'

'Don't really know. She just disappeared. We came home from school one day and she was gone. Took the mad aunty with her – and my sister ran away and my dad tried to kill the Iranian boy who'd lived with us forever. Then he – my dad – kidnapped us and brought us over here, where they could never find us.'

'Geez – and I thought I had crazy parents. You win.'

'I miss her so much – every day, I miss her.'

The tears came unexpectedly and Anya swung into a side street and stopped the car. She reached over and grabbed my hand and I clasped hers. The seat was slippery with sweat and the car made a ticking noise. We put our arms around each other and cried and blew our noses and used up a whole box of tissues. The sun spread over our bare skin and the remnants of a headache started up again behind my eyes. As I had done with Gloria, we checked each other after the storm, straightened our clothes, wiped our faces and patted down our hair. Then she took me home.

Thirteen

The fat man was the Historian's friend, but the Magician adopted him as one of her lost causes. We had to call him Anand Uncle and put up with him on Sunday afternoons when he came to have lunch with us and go for a ride in the Historian's police jeep afterwards. When Gloria complained about his large belches and the way he scratched his armpits, the Magician shook her head at her.

'How many times should I explain that everyone who eats a meal in this house is destined to do so?' The Magician was stern and Gloria fell back. 'On every grain of rice is written the name of the person who will eat it. We cannot complain about the people who eat with us – you know that. Yes, I know his manners are a little strange, but what can you expect from a man without a wife and daughters?' The Magician sighed and added, 'I believe his mother lives with him but she is quite a *junglee* – a peasant from some village who hasn't taught the poor man anything.'

'But why should we have to put up with him?' Gloria flipped her hair over one shoulder and stamped her foot. 'Why can't the Historian look after him? Why do you have to? You never do anything with us. You're always looking after disgusting people like him and Meher Aunty.'

'Disgusting,' I repeated. 'Disgusting *junglee* peasant.'

'That's enough, Maryam. You can either stay and help me or go away.' The Magician's mouth took on that familiar straight line, and Gloria pulled me out of the kitchen by my arm.

'Yes,' agreed Sohrab later when I complained about what the Magician had said to us. 'I think this is what all Iranian mothers do: they like to feed people. Even when we say we don't want to eat any more, still they keep on giving us more. I'm very happy you told Farah *khanum* about my problem with rice. Now I have no stomach pain at night. Thank you, Maryam.'

'You're welcome. But the Magician's not Iranian – she's Indian. Her mother was born in Iran. She's never been there so how can she be Iranian?' I had this discussion with Sohrab often and wondered if he was a bit slow. He seemed to think my mother was a foreigner like him.

'Maryam,' Sohrab took off his glasses and wiped them before looking at my shoulder and smiling. 'If I stay here and marry a nice *khanum*, after thirty years I will still be Iranian and my children will be Iranian even if they never go to Iran. Like you. Like...' he blushed and said 'Gloria' and put his glasses back on.

'So what about the Historian?' I wasn't done yet. I'd had enough of my mongrel ancestry and people arguing over who we really were. 'Do I now go around telling people I'm Anglo-Iranian instead of Anglo-Indian?'

'No, Maryam.' Sohrab started walking with me towards the pond. 'Say you are unique – you are world citizen. Now let us go and talk to the fat man so your mum can have some peace, yes?' He giggled and pulled out a squashed cigarette from his pocket, squinting into the mid-morning sun.

Anand's mother was a strict vegetarian who did not allow meat to be cooked in her son's house. So on Sundays we ate a lot of dead things in honour of our guest: goat curry, fried fish, chicken tikka, brain masala and, on one occasion, a whole roasted partridge brought in by the driver's son from his hunt. After lunch, the Historian would take Anand for a ride in his police jeep and they would be gone for two or three hours. They always returned in high spirits, smelling of unfamiliar scents, demanding cups of tea and samosas, which the Magician served with averted eyes and tightly buttoned mouth. Gloria and I begged to be taken along for one of these rides, and the Historian would wink and say, 'Next week, eh?' We were teenagers before we realised we were never going for that ride.

When the Historian swapped his police jeep for a brand-new red Fiat, the afternoon rides stopped and Anand stretched out on a long divan and snored with his mouth open until the Magician woke him at four pm to serve tea. Gloria hated Anand Uncle more than I did. She said he was a fat pig, using the forbidden word *suwar* deliberately, while I hushed her with round eyes and a finger on my lips. She said that she was sure the Magician was being forced to look after him against her wishes and that we should 'do something'.

'Like what?'

'Hold a pillow over his head while he sleeps. I can hold the pillow and you can tie his feet together. That should fix him. He probably won't die but he'll be scared.'

'Gloria – you've been reading too many Agatha Christie books. Why do you hate him so much?'

'I told you. He's a pig. He smells and burps and makes our mother feed him all day. He has fat fingers and he's a bad man. A very bad man. Stay away from him, Hannah.'

'I don't hear the Magician complaining. I think she likes him.'

Gloria dug her fingers hard into my shoulders and shook me. 'You don't know anything,' she said tearfully as I tried to wrench out of her grasp.

In the next instant we held on to each other and cried. I cried because I could still feel her fingers squeezing into the soft parts of my neck and shoulders and I was more scared than hurt. I don't know why she cried.

Anand Uncle came every week until the Magician disappeared. She left on a Friday and he came on his usual Sunday when the Historian was throwing things around and cursing loudly. Arriving in the middle of this chaos, Anand looked around as if he expected someone to provide a rational explanation. The Historian yelled 'Bastard!' when he saw him and threw a tattered hardbound copy of *David Copperfield* at him, which he caught smartly and put down on the table near the library door.

My brothers advised me to go to my room, Clive trying to drag me away from my post at the door. He gave up when I refused to budge, and stood beside me, watching the Historian and Anand exchange abuse and flying objects.

'Why doesn't he just leave?' I whispered to Clive, 'the *suwar*, I mean?'

'Hannah, don't use that word. You know how the Magician hates it.'

'She's not here, is she? So, why doesn't Suwar Uncle just go away instead of arguing with the Historian?'

'None of our business. Please, Hannah, let's go. Why are you doing this?'

We never saw Anand again. Before we left for Perth, we heard that he had committed suicide by lying down on the train tracks near his house. According to the servants who took his mother back to her village, his body was cut neatly into three – head severed, body wedged between the tracks with arms beside the headless body, legs cut off at the knees. When they found him, blood was still spurting from the limbs. Gloria said (with a look in her eyes that reminded me of the Magician) that bad people deserved to die horrible deaths. The Historian's comment on the demise of his long-term friend and companion of Sunday lunches and jeep rides: 'Good riddance to bad rubbish.'

Fourteen

We were good at adopting strays and assimilating them into the chaos that passed for the Historian's household. We weren't that good at being adopted or assimilated ourselves. We found this out when the Magician disappeared. The Historian went quiet. He locked himself inside the library and ignored us. Meher Aunty shouted at the servants and cooked dal and rice every afternoon. No more biryani and chelo kebabs for us. Our brothers looked uncomfortable when we cried. The girls at school whispered and giggled when they saw us, and Gloria had to sit outside Sister Angelina's office for pulling a senior girl's hair. Then I got into trouble for calling Shalini a *kutti*, which sounded so much worse than calling her a bitch in English. We stopped going to school. No one noticed.

Gloria and I went to the rose patch every morning and sat in the lower branches of the mango tree. Without the Magician, my clothes were tatty and dirty, and I'd started raiding Gloria's. They didn't fit me yet and I was ashamed of my appearance, especially when Meher Aunty looked at my chest and muttered curses. Gloria always looked nice – the aunties had once said it wouldn't matter if they flung a sack at her, she would still look like an angel. Today she wore jeans and a handloom kurta. The Historian had banned her from wearing dresses after she'd turned sixteen.

'We're orphans now, Hannah,' Gloria said. 'And don't say we still have a father.'

'She's not dead. She'll come back for us.'

'What if he kills us first?'

'He won't,' I said, patting Gloria's hand and swallowing bile.

She worried me. She was broody and difficult and I didn't know what to make of her. I had spirited away the journals from the library before the Historian laid siege to it. The Magician's sketchbooks and those green hardcover journals were now hidden inside the wardrobe I shared with Gloria. My shelves bulged with the remnants of an absent mother as I tried to steal her back – squirrelling away things she had worn, touched, discarded. She had not taken much, so it was easy to lay claim to a dupatta, a sari, a ring, a torn photo…an unfinished school cardigan.

'Rani,' Gloria said. 'She took Rani and not us. Rani is a grown-up. We are children – or at least you are a child even if I'm not. What am I supposed to do with you?'

I hugged her. 'You don't have to do anything, Gloria. You'll see – she'll come back. She just needs to find somewhere to hide us. Then she'll come and get us. Anyway, Clive and Warren are grown-ups too, and they'll know what to do.'

'Oh, yes,' Gloria said in her new nasty voice. 'Scaredy-cat Clive will protect us and Lord Warren will climb down from his tower to rescue us, I'm sure. You keep on believing that, my little infant.'

Gloria was right. Neither brother had shown any interest in looking after us even though Clive scooped me into an embrace when he saw me slouching around the house, eyeing the library. Warren walked around with pink-rimmed eyes and smelled of cheap whisky. He came home late at night and stumbled through the house till Clive or Sohrab put him to bed.

And we were never going to be rid of Meher Aunty. 'Think of me as your mother now,' she'd said the day after she ordered the servants to break open the lock on the attic door with a stone. 'No point in wasting this room. We can use it as a storeroom. Growing children eat a lot. We need to buy dal and rice and wheat in bulk.'

'You are not our mother,' Gloria mumbled, and I squeezed her hand and repeated loudly, 'Gloria says you are not our mother. You aren't anybody's mother.'

Meher Aunty put down the low cane stool she was carrying and slapped me across the face so hard I staggered. 'Open your mouth again in my presence and I will close it permanently, you little half-breed,' she said, waving her large pink hand in front of my face, and Gloria wiped droplets of blood from my lips and dragged me away.

We heard shouts from the house and jumped down from the mango tree, clasped hands and ran towards the sounds. The Historian was in the courtyard, kicking a small pile of books. Our brothers were arguing with him but he ignored them. I ran to Clive, who caught me swiftly and shook his head. The Historian came out of the library with more books that he threw on the pile. They were the Magician's books – *Lorna Doone*, *Little Women*, *Fear of Flying*, *Edible Gardens*, *Gitanjali*, *Shahnama* and curly-scripted books of Farsi poetry. The Historian poured petrol over them out of a square tin can and lit a match. The next instant they went up in flames and I retched. Clive held me.

Fifteen

The Historian was losing his hair and it made him obsessive about his appearance. He massaged his scalp with almond oil before he showered and stroked the remaining strands with a wide-toothed comb. Every morning, in front of the gilt-framed mirror, he patted down his scant hair before scowling and turning away. One of his women friends told him yoga was good for hair growth. He bought a book on yoga and started doing headstands.

My brothers and I learned to live with the sight of the Historian standing on his head in his underpants. In the kitchen every morning, we looked at each other and the nearly naked Historian by the sink, slicking back his hair. 'Two birds with one stone,' he said cheerfully. 'Yoga for posture and for hair.'

Warren was especially bold. 'I don't think yoga is going to get rid of your pot belly, Dad. All that cheese and fruit and wine in your diet makes you sluggish. Downside of living in wine country, I suppose. You need some regular exercise. You should come for a run with me in the morning. It'll be fun.'

'Are you being cheeky, boy?' The Historian glared at Warren, who smiled back and picked up a banana from the fruit bowl.

Warren was six feet tall with an impressive chest. He worked out at the gym and ran on the beach with tanned blond women. Clive was equally tall and broad-chested, but less inclined to rile the Historian the way Warren did. My handsome brothers – the Magician (and Gloria) should see them now.

Warren chucked a banana peel in the bin and turned around. 'Of course not,' he said. 'Only trying to help – works for me, as you can see. I eat what I want and run for an hour.' He laid a hand on his flat stomach and winked.

The Historian frowned. 'What do you think, Hannah? Have I lost some weight or not? I feel lighter, you know. And certainly hair loss has stopped.'

Warren sniggered and the Historian's eyes bulged.

'Warren's right. You should go running with him in the morning. It'll help.' *You might have a heart attack and die and then we can all go back to India to find the Magician.* I thought I'd said it out loud when the kitchen went quiet. I looked up to meet Clive's thoughtful gaze. The flyscreen door slid open and the Historian and Warren went out, still arguing; Warren's voice was edged with laughter.

'Watch it, Hannah,' Clive said, putting an arm around me. 'One of these days you'll say it out loud. Wishing him dead won't kill him. It'll only make him more determined to outlive us all. How are you going anyway, with your studies and things?'

'Isn't your house nearly ready, Clive? I can't wait to move in with you and Leanne. My only other option is Anya, and she doesn't have much money. I have a feeling I'll end up paying for everything if I live with her. Much better to sponge off my brother instead, don't you think? I'm not staying another minute here after you're gone.'

Clive tugged at my hair, shorter now that I didn't have Gloria's patience to comb and braid it every morning. 'I'm counting on you. You're almost as good a cook as your mother – and that's saying something. Of course you can live with us. Now, do you want a lift to your crazy friend's place? You really need to get your licence, Hannah. You can't rely on us to drive you around forever. I don't know which is worse – seeing Anya drive like a maniac or you refusing to drive at all. What is it with girls and cars? Get your licence and your independence. What's wrong with that?'

'Teach me or pay for my lessons,' I grinned, and picked up my bag and books.

∞

I spent as much time as I could in Anya's house, coming home only when I knew my brothers would be there. Clive was engaged to Leanne, a friendly Australian girl who liked me enough to agree that I could live with them if I paid board and helped with the chores. Leanne's parents had an old rental place in Wembley that they'd sold to Clive and Leanne at mate's rates. Her dad was a carpenter and had done most of the renovation himself, with Clive helping him on weekends and evenings. It was now ready for us — we were going to move in a couple of weeks and the Historian was trying to think of ways to prevent us.

'What's the hurry, eh?' he asked repeatedly, whenever we gathered in the kitchen. 'What am I going to do in this big house all by myself? Warren thinks it's a bloody hotel – don't you, eh? Just use the facilities and leave. But when we're all here – like this, it's good. Why do you want the burden of a house and all that expense when you should be out enjoying yourself, Clive? If you must live with that girl, why not live here? There's plenty of room. You can convert the sleep-out into a nice space for both of you. Think about it – and our tradition. Boys live in the ancestral home.'

'I'm twenty-five years old, Dad,' Clive said. 'I can't live with you forever. Don't use that Indian argument about joint families again. We're not living in India. We don't have an ancestral home – you sold it, remember? And that girl happens to be my fiancée. You won't even say her name and you want her to live here?'

'You brought us here. You didn't ask if that's what we wanted,' Warren added, as he usually did. 'When in Rome...'

The Historian stared at us, blue eyes blank and steady. 'All right, have it your own way, but don't say I didn't try to guide you. Five minutes in this country and you want to embrace their unsustainable lifestyle – rushing to get into debt, buying things you can't pay for. You know what I owe on this house? Nothing. Zero dollars. And how much are you borrowing for your house?

Tell me. Just because the bank is foolish enough to give you a loan doesn't mean anything. Bankers here are stupid – they'll lend money to anyone. What will happen if you lose your job and you can't pay it back? Don't come to me when they repossess – you're paying too much for that falling-down old house anyway.'

'I'm not arguing with you, Dad. Thanks for dinner, Hannah.'

We stood up, my brothers and I, and gathered up pots and plates and carried them into the kitchen. Clive stacked the dishwasher and Warren prowled around, opening the pantry door, looking inside the fridge – he was always hungry. The Magician would have given him a glass of sweet almond milk, sprinkled with saffron. *Growing boys need proper food.* She would have made tea with mint and lemon for us. *Scrape a little bit of ginger in the tea for warmth.* She would have loved this house with its purple trees and laughing birds and vigorous light. *We need two sets of curtains, one for winter and one for summer.* She would have walked to the bench overlooking the river at the back of the old church with her sketchbook, listening and smiling. *It's so peaceful here. I can hear birds and trees and the river flowing around the bend.* She would have hugged me and said she couldn't believe I was old enough to cook, work, study, drive a car and live on my own. *How did you grow up so quickly?* She would have held me and wondered about Gloria. *I should have noticed and taken better care of her.* She would have regretted taking in Sohrab. *The snake in the garden.*

Sixteen

I wish I hadn't seen them.

Just as I wish I hadn't seen the Historian with the woman all those years ago, when I was five. Gloria had carried me away from the library window then with a finger on her lips. She'd said, 'You didn't see anything, did you, Hannah? You know you'll get into big trouble if you saw something?' I hadn't seen anything, I agreed. I tried to believe it. But dreams don't lie. And I saw them over and over again – the woman clutching her sari in handfuls close to her chest, head down, long hair falling over her face and the Historian, smiling, eyes closed.

A month after the Historian torched my mother's books, I sat by the pond where the *mali* filled his watering cans every morning for the Magician's herb garden. I couldn't be seen from the house and no one came here except the gardener. When I heard voices, I ducked behind the wall of the pond. Gloria and Sohrab. I stayed hidden but squirmed forward till I could see their legs. They wore jeans – Gloria barefoot and Sohrab in his old moccasins. A cigarette butt, still smouldering, landed near my hands.

'I am not mad,' Sohrab sounded furious. 'And what I have said is not funny – so you will please stop laughing. How can you think this is funny?'

'Sorry, Sohrab, I'm not laughing at you. You know that. I'm just nervous. I don't think it'll work. I'm only seventeen.'

What was Gloria nervous about? I wanted to see her face now, but Sohrab's thick voice cut into the afternoon again.

'Yes, and I am twenty-two. We are old enough. It can work. I promise...'

Sohrab's foot reached out towards the cigarette stub and crushed it against the gravel. He coughed and flicked his lighter several times. Dust and smoke drifted into my nostrils and I hoped I wouldn't sneeze. Sohrab's shoes made a scraping, rustling sound. He always shuffled. Gloria I couldn't hear at all.

They were quiet for so long I thought they had gone. I peered over the edge of the wall. They were still there. Sohrab had one hand on Gloria's bum; the other held a fresh cigarette. Gloria's arms were around his neck and her head was on his shoulder. They were almost the same height. Sohrab's hand massaged Gloria's bum and lifted her kurta away from the waistband of her jeans. The hand found her bra strap and lingered over the fastening. Gloria wriggled and moved his hand away from her back and placed it around her waist again. They leapt apart as I stood up.

'Hannah,' Gloria's eyebrows came together in a deep frown and Sohrab turned pink.

I looked back at them and knew that all was finally lost. I was alone.

The Historian was in the library and I didn't knock. I went in and stared at him as he lifted an eyebrow.

'Not now, Hannah. Whatever it is, I don't want to know,' he said. His voice was hoarse as if he had been shouting.

'Sohrab touched Gloria,' I said. 'He touched her everywhere. He said he loved her, but not like a brother. She's only seventeen. Sorry to have disturbed you. I thought I should tell you.'

The Historian's extensive vocabulary of Hindi/English swear words streamed from his mouth as he ransacked Sohrab's room. *Haramzada kamina suwar chor bastard.* He threw out clothes, books, papers, cigarettes, photographs, shoes, a radio and that chair the Magician used to sit on. He kicked the frame of Sohrab's bed and tore up the pen-circled map of Iran on the wall. He made a pile of everything he could remove and I wondered how long it would take to burn the clothes. But this time my brothers intervened. Clive picked up Sohrab's things and Warren went next door to ask old Mrs D'Silva for help.

Mrs D'Silva tut-tutted and put her hand on the Historian's arm. 'Gordon, my boy,' she said gently. 'First you must stop using this dirty language in front of the children. Then you must come with me – right now – you must come. Come and sit down with Mr D'Silva and have a drink to calm you down. I will sort this out, don't you worry.' She led him away, holding his arm and smiling at him as if he were a child having a tantrum.

I refused to look at Gloria when she joined us in the courtyard. Clive put his arm around my shoulders and said, 'Okay, kids, listen. This is becoming ridiculous. We've got to stick together and stop him. He doesn't have to be in charge any more. We can be in charge.'

'Okay, Sergeant Clive,' Gloria said. 'What do you think we should do? I don't really care. I have a plan and it doesn't include any of you, especially not Little Miss Tattle-Tale here. Congratulations, Hannah. You've ruined my life. The Magician did the right thing. Why on earth would anyone willingly live with a bunch of *suwars* like you?'

Meher Aunty crept up behind us and fastened her fingers on my arm. I shook her free and she glared at me, black eyes round with venom. 'I should slap your faces – all of you – standing here and using filthy language. Have you learned nothing? All my hard work over all these years – all down the drain. See, this is what happens when you don't know whose blood is flowing in your veins. No wonder she ran away. But why she took that madwoman with her and left me alone with you all – who knows?'

'Shut up!' Gloria shouted. Her face was scary, angry, wet. 'You fat, meddlesome frog. We're not dead yet and you are nobody. You are nobody. I know everything, you horrible old woman. I know what you did. It's your fault she's gone. You filled her head with your rubbish. Keep your fat hands away from us or I swear I'll strangle you in your sleep.' Gloria was so loud even Warren looked scared. I covered my ears with my hands.

'Where did you learn the language of the filthy bazaar, you wicked girl? Is this what we taught you?' Meher's voice was vicious and her fat hand was advancing towards Gloria when she stopped as if she had been jerked back by a puppet-master.

'You heard her,' the Historian said, appearing in that way he had that never allowed us a moment to relax, never released us from the bind of nightmares, of bedwetting. Omnipresent. I used to shudder at that word when we chanted our prayers at school before assembly. How could God be omnipresent and loving, if that meant being everywhere, all the time, always? 'You heard my child,' he continued, looking at Meher. 'She sounds like she wants to kill you and I won't stop her. You better get out of my house while you still can.'

We scattered quickly, away from each other, ashamed.

Seventeen

The first time I met Gabriel, he was elbow deep in sawdust, sneezing loudly and blowing his nose into a once-clean hanky. Bent over a large black plastic bag filled with sawdust and wood shavings, hands and arms plunged into its depths, he muttered small curses and agitated the dust that settled on him like brown snowflakes.

I watched from the door as he straightened up holding a small round object and said, 'Gotcha, little bugger.' Then, his right hand over his eyes to peer at me, he sneezed loudly again and said, 'Oh, heck. How long have you been there? Come in, please. I've lost a router bit in there somewhere.' He stamped his feet, whacked his chest with his hands and came towards me, trailing curls of wood and smelling of smoke, a tall man with green eyes and laughter in his voice. 'What can I do you for?' He offered me a warm, dusty hand and gripped mine firmly in exchange.

'Oh,' I said. 'A friend recommended you. You make furniture – to order?'

'Certainly do. What are you after? I don't do cheap stuff, but we can haggle over prices later.' He was covered in wood shavings and I wanted to reach out and brush a curl off his tanned arm. I sucked in my breath.

'Oh, it's not for me. My brother's just moved into a new house and I'm sponging off him for a bit, so I thought I'd get him something good as a housewarming present.'

'Geez, you're a nice sister.' He laughed, eyes crinkling at the corners, his voice filling spaces left by an absent mother, sister, country. 'Let me show you what I've got and you can tell me what you have in mind.'

He led me through the workshop into a gleaming gallery dominated by a giant grandfather clock made entirely from jarrah, which he said had taken him three years to build. The price tag on it was $45,000 and he grinned at my raised eyebrows, saying, 'Priced so no one buys it, hopefully! But hey, if someone wants to pay that much they can have it. It'll knock years off my mortgage, and think what I could do with all that extra space.'

He seemed so foreign. Everything about him – the wide shoulders, that T-shirt with a Vegemite logo, the dusty boots and the baggy Levi's, that laugh, those eyes – everything felt foreign. Everything I'd taught myself about Australians didn't help me with him. He looked at me appraisingly, boldly, as if he knew my knocking heart, my scattered speech, my apologetic eyes. I wanted to lean into his embrace and kiss that smiling mouth. None of our future encounters would equal that moment in shifting sunlight when desire for a stranger knotted shamelessly in my stomach.

'A clock would be nice,' I said through dry lips. 'Not this mortgage-buster clock, of course. Do you have anything smaller?'

'Walk this way.' Gabriel placed his hand on my arm briefly and steered me towards a shelf at the far end of the gallery. Among hand-turned jarrah bowls and scrolled tea chests, there was a clock. It was a little rocking chair with a pair of lovebirds holding up a round clock face. Gabriel touched the tiny chair and it rocked gently for a few seconds. It was perfect: pale brown, deftly carved and probably unaffordable.

I smoothed a fingertip over the base. 'How much?' I asked.

'Whatever you want to pay,' he replied.

'I have no idea. Please, I'd like to buy it and you need to give me a price.'

'Twenty bucks okay?'

'You're not serious?' My eyes ached with the effort of holding his amused gaze. I looked at the price tags on the bowls. There was nothing under one hundred dollars on the shelf.

'Look.' Gabriel brushed something off my shoulder and took the clock off the shelf. 'Do you want it or not? I haven't got all day to stand around and talk to pretty girls. No one has looked at it and it's been sitting on that shelf for months. It took me ages to make. I don't do fussy little things like this any more. Twenty bucks and it's yours. And if you think you're robbing me, how about you buy me a cup of coffee? Deal?' He blew on my chair-clock, fished out a rag from the pocket of his jeans and wiped the base before handing it to me.

I gave him the money, then walked with him to the little cafe next to the gallery and ordered two coffees. He sat by the window and watched me. When the coffee arrived, he said, 'Now, tell me everything, Hannah Roper. What do you do when you're not supporting local woodworkers? Where are you from?'

I don't remember what I said. I was distracted by his eyes.

I never gave the clock to Clive and Leanne. I saved up for a month and gave them an Ikea voucher instead. Leanne was thrilled and bought a square lamp table, two plastic chairs, a couple of cushions and six long-stemmed wine glasses. She didn't notice the little clock next to the Magician's photo on my desk.

Eighteen

The week after the Magician left, Sohrab became a communist but continued to wear the *taveez* she had given him before absconding. He said he didn't believe in religion, particularly Islam. The ayatollahs had ruined his country and he didn't have time for Islam any more. He touched his *taveez* and told me he would look after me. Even if his country had gone to the dogs he would not fail in his duty to us.

'I must go back, Maryam,' he said, when the Magician disappeared. 'But of course I will wait until she returns. She will come back. She will have plan for you. She is good mother. Please don't worry. *We* will look after you.'

I sat on the Magician's chair in his room and swung my feet. I wanted to believe him. He kept looking at the door and chewed his fingernails. He took off his glasses and blinked a few times; his eyelashes were as long and curly as a girl's. I wasn't supposed to be sitting alone in the room with him. The Magician said although he was like our brother, we still had to behave like good girls from an honourable family: keep our distance but show him affection. Meher Aunty had given me the lecture: boys only look for one thing from a girl – only one thing, mind you – and that is the only thing girls must keep safe. Especially motherless half-breeds like us.

'She used to talk to you in Farsi,' I said. 'Did she say anything that might help us find her? Do you think she's gone to Iran?'

'I don't know, Maryam. Yes, we talk about Iran, the streets, the parks, the food. She ask about my family – Maman *jun* and Baba and my brothers. I tell her about Roohi *jun* who is engaged to that animal – if he touches one hair on her head, I kill him.' Sohrab chewed his lower lip and murmured an apology.

'It's okay, Sohrab.' He spoke of Roohi often. She was his sister, his only sister, and Sohrab and his seven brothers had sworn to make the unfortunate Ali's life a living hell if he made their sister unhappy. I wished Clive and Warren loved us like that. 'What else did you talk about?'

'I think she miss her parents. She cannot remember them and this makes her sad. She never tell me anything private. And I don't know where or why she is gone.' Sohrab stood up and pulled out a suitcase from the top of the wardrobe. He hunted for something and then handed me a round object, wrapped in a long silky scarf. 'This is all I have. She give me this – but you can have it.'

I unwrapped the scarf and looked at the green papier-mâché box I had seen dozens of times in the Magician's room, next to other similar boxes holding objects she might have a use for someday. I knew what she kept in this one. Buttons, beads, knitted squares of wool she used as patterns for our cardigans. What an odd, sad thing to give to Sohrab. He nodded as if he read my mind.

'She will come back. Please believe me. She will come and I will go. I will find Baba and Maman and then I will come back here. You must be strong, Maryam. You are good girl.'

I took the box and hugged Sohrab. Meher Aunty had a filthy mind. He was our brother, like Clive and Warren. A better brother. He and Gloria often had their heads together, talking softly, matching steps as they walked to the market, always bringing something back for me. He smelled of Brut aftershave these days and his hair was neater. Gloria had persuaded him to buy blue jeans and T-shirts, and he didn't look too different from my brothers now.

A fair exchange, I thought – the Magician would come back and Sohrab could leave. I took his glasses off, polished them with the edge of my kurta and placed them crookedly back on his nose. I tried to return the scarf but he said I could keep that too.

Nineteen

Anya persuaded me to share a flat with her after all. I'd been living with Clive and Leanne for six months when she begged me to move in with her. She was renting in Maylands, in a building where students on minimal budgets ate canned tuna and drank Coke from recyclable bottles. The flat was awful: stained carpets, smell of grease in the kitchen, flaking paint in the bathroom. 'Come on, it's a rite of passage,' she said. 'This is what girls do. They share flats and boyfriends and clothes. I can't pay the rent on my own and I don't want to ask my crazy parents for anything. Please, Hannah?'

I caved in. Clive and Leanne's white cottage with shiny floors felt like home in a way the Historian's house never had. I had a tiny room in the back that looked out on a gnarled grapevine and I was happy. Clive was the kindest of us all. He had inherited the Magician's relaxed empathy, her willingness to give others a second chance.

At first it was great. Anya was generous with lifts to and from university, waiting for me if I had a class even if she didn't. We shopped at second-hand stores and she pointed out styles she thought might suit me. We went to the movies together on half-price Tuesdays. I told myself I wasn't trying to replace Gloria, but it was so good to have a girl share my life again. To hang out underwear without checking for the presence of boys, to include tampons on the shopping list, to sprawl inelegantly on the couch and not worry about leaving hair on the bathroom floor. Occasionally her possessiveness irked me, but she lost interest in me when she started dating Chris Wong. Chris was our senior at university, doing English with us that semester. He was from Malaysia and said he was used to girls like me. I took it as a compliment and invited him to dinner whenever I cooked a curry. He drove a Land Cruiser, which came in handy when the rich people along the river threw out their sofas and fridges. We furnished our flat with their discards – mismatched chairs, a dining table, a couch and an armchair, a bar fridge and a desk. Friends chipped in with odds and ends, and Gabriel promised to make a bookshelf. My first stab at independent living looked like a scene from *The Pickwick Papers*.

Anya draped herself over Chris whenever he spent time at the flat, forcing me to look away from what their hands were doing, and complained about him when he left.

'He's got BO. Pongs like a Chinese fish market. Thinks he's special because he's rich. We'll keep him till the flat's fully furnished, then get rid of him.'

'That's mean, Anya,' I said. 'He's polite and he doesn't take advantage of you. Buy him some deodorant.'

'Don't be so naive,' Anya snapped. 'Which century do you live in? Doesn't take advantage of me, my arse – just because you're playing Elizabeth Bennet to Mr Darcy, you think all boys are like your sexy Gabriel.'

The Magician would have called Anya temperamental. She wasn't like my Australian friends at school or the quiet Indian girls with whom the Historian had insisted I make friends when we first arrived. Aunty Frankie's girls, my new cousins, were easy to be with. You knew if you had upset them; they told you. You knew when you had done something to make them happy; they flung their arms around you and called you a sweetie.

Anya's signals were confusing. She went from happy to foul in an instant, then switched back again. I sniffed the flat for an inkling of her mood when I came back at the end of the day. Sometimes the house smelled of chemicals and sometimes of flowers. She ate an astonishing amount of junk, and littered the flat with empty packets of salt-and-vinegar chips, squashed Coke tins and flimsy items of clothing. She had no concept of privacy, walking in when I was in the shower to talk to me about something that could have waited till I finished. When she ran out of clean clothes she helped herself to mine. We argued.

'I can't believe I gave up a nice clean house to live in this dump with you,' I said one evening after coming home to Anya sprawled on the couch with empty takeaway containers and a Walkman plugged into her ear. She ignored me and I leaned over and pulled the plugs off.

'What's your problem?' she screamed.

'You're the problem. I did not sign up for this. I've had enough. I'm going back to my brother's.'

Anya stared, then stood up and flung her arms around me. 'I'm so sorry. I can be such a pain sometimes. My friggin' mother's been calling and doing my head in, but that's no excuse. Look, I'll clean up and try to do better, I promise. I know you're a bit of a neat freak and I'm just a slob.'

I disentangled myself from her embrace and patted her arm. She whizzed around the flat with a vacuum cleaner and threw a big pile of clothes in the wash. In an hour the flat was tidy, with fresh flowers in a glass on the kitchen bench and the smell of pine disinfectant in the sink. We ordered pizza for dinner and Anya insisted on paying, because she'd been such a friggin' pest.

Anya deferred her studies for a semester. She kept her evening job at Chicken Treat and bought several blank canvases and tubes of paint. She had an urge to paint, she said. She'd always done well at art in school, she said. She made some desultory splotches on a canvas one weekend and I never saw her look at it again. The artistic desire went the same way as her other urges – washing clothes or tidying up or asking to borrow my clothes.

Regardless of weather, she started wearing leggings and black lipstick, denim skirts and tank tops inscribed with band names like My Bloody Valentine and The Jesus and Mary Chain. Pictures of skinny boys with frizzy hair and black jeans appeared on the insides of all the kitchen cabinets, stuck on with Blu-Tack. Even though the agent never checked inside our cupboards on rent inspection day, I protested. 'You know we're not allowed to stick things on walls and cupboards. We'll lose our bond when we leave. Anyway, what's the point of putting the same picture inside every cupboard?'

'Here, listen to this – it's awesome,' she said, turning the sound up on the Walkman and offering it to me. When I shook my head she put her arms over her head and swayed, singing, '*Psychocandy, baby, wind screaming around the trees, baby.*'

'Oh, how very mature of you,' I said. 'How old are you again?'

'*Talk in rhyme with my chaotic soul, baby.*'

'I'm not going to talk to you at all while you're being an idiot.'

A large silver cross bumped against her chest as she jumped up and down and tried to get me to join her. Chris, who had dropped in to see if we wanted to watch a video, laughed. She narrowed her eyes and aimed a small kick at him, saying, 'Feck off, cretin.'

'Oh, grow up, Anya, and pick your stuff up off the floor. I'm not your mother.' I turned my back on her and wondered how I was going to get out of our rental agreement.

'She's definitely crazy,' Gabriel said to me when I told him about the music and the clothes and the fake accent. 'You know, she sounds like she could be on something. Thought about that?'

I absorbed this comment in silence before asking, 'Like what? What's she on?'

'Stronger than weed for sure. Maybe she's into the hard stuff.'

'Come on, Gabriel, if she was doing heroin I think I'd know. I haven't seen needles lying around or puncture marks on her arms.'

'What about bottles? Pills? Powders? Smells in the bath after she's used it? Could be anything – or she could be naturally loopy and in no need of chemical help.'

∞

Gabriel was right. Anya had pills for everything – period pain, headaches, gastro, something mysterious she couldn't tell me about. She popped pills all day. Sometimes I pretended not to see her drink vodka straight from the bottle. Her appetite was vigorous and she still ate everything I cooked with enthusiasm. Like the Magician, I had believed that if you ate well you were healthy.

I came home one evening after a late class and found the front door open. Chris was on his knees beside Anya on the floor. Her eyes were open and her head was on a cushion. A dribble of spit ran down the side of her mouth.

'Oh, thank God you're here.' Chris looked terrified. 'I found her like this. Should I call an ambulance? Hannah, has this happened before? She can't hear me.'

I knelt down and touched Anya's forehead, then picked up her limp hand and rubbed it. I had no idea what to do but it seemed to calm Chris. Anya's face was damp, and the cotton top she was wearing was damp too. I kept rubbing her hands and she blinked, shifted her gaze to me and said, 'What're you doing? Trying to crush my hand?'

'What happened, Anya?'

'Dunno. Must've passed out. I had a headache this morning. Jesus friggin' Christ, I need a drink – tell Rice Boy there to get me some water.'

Chris's face twisted. 'You crazy bitch!' he said, red spots flaring on his high cheekbones. 'I hope you die.'

Anya snatched her hand from mine and launched herself at Chris, her fingers digging into his neck while she screamed. Chris's head snapped back and he looked as if he was choking. He pushed and I pulled, loosening her fingers from around his neck. She kept screaming and I thumped her hard on her back. She burst into tears and loosened her grip. We forced her into a chair and looked at each other over her head. She slumped forward, hair over her face, whimpering.

'I'll call my brother,' I said to Chris. 'Clive will know what to do.'

Chris nodded and rubbed his neck.

∞

Clive drove us to Charles Gairdner Hospital. When we got there, I called Anya's parents. The tired intern explained that she needed to be kept in overnight for tests. 'She's severely dehydrated,' he said with a yawn. 'We need to put her on a saline drip. Maybe a stomach pump. If she has relatives, you should call them. We can't do anything until they sign some papers. You guys are friends, right?'

'Don't call my crazy mother,' Anya whispered. 'She'll tell Dad and he'll kill me. Please stay, Hannah. Don't leave me alone.'

'I'm sorry, Anya. I've already called. They're on their way.'

'Get lost, bitch.'

'Anya, please listen. What's going on? I can't live with you if you're going to scare us all like this.'

'Feck off. Leave me alone.'

∞

Her mother arrived in a taxi and sat beside Anya's trolley-bed. 'You no look after her,' she said to me, face firm with reproach. 'I trust you with my beautiful girl. I give you food and coffee in my home. Look what you do. The father – he kill you. He love his little girl.'

Clive put his arm around my shoulders. 'There's no need for talk like that,' he said. 'My sister saved Anya's life. Come on, Hannah, let's go.'

'But…'

'Hannah, there's no need to drag this out. Your friend needs help and you've done all you can. Come, now.'

I moved my things out of the flat that night and into Clive's spare room. Propped up against Anya's photo in the lounge room, I left a month's rent money in an envelope.

Sliding into sleep later, I dreamed. The Historian was a bearded goat who nibbled at my feet and covered them with a silk scarf. A skinny girl wearing black lipstick laughed and died. The Magician dropped cool liquids down my throat and the Historian carried me to the old house against the hills, trailing blood and muscle.

'Hannah, wake up. Here, have some water.' Clive and Leanne bent over my bed, their hands gentle on my body, voices soft and low.

Gloria.

Forgive me.

Twenty

Three years before the Magician abandoned us, she led me to *that* room and told me she was going to have a secret party for me. I wasn't to say anything to anyone. It was a special secret – between her and me and fat Aunty Meher.

'But, Ammi, why Meher Aunty? I don't like her. She's mean. She's always calling us names. And why can't we tell Gloria?'

'Gloria has already had her secret party. You'll understand when you grow up, Maryam. This is how it is for girls. Meher Aunty knows these things, so please don't be rude.'

'What things, Ammi? And please, please ask Gloria.'

The Magician didn't reply. She ruffled my hair absently and pulled me close to her for an instant before I saw her wet eyes. Her arms were cool around my ears. When I shrugged myself free, she smiled a tight smile, the same smile she used when she wanted to tell us something she knew we wouldn't like. I looked around.

The storeroom at the back of the house was filled with things too broken to use and too good to throw out. We used to play here, Gloria and I, until she refused to come in one day, a week after her twelfth birthday, saying it was haunted and a *djinn* would get us. It looked the same as always, and I turned to ask the Magician if I could have it as my room instead of sharing with Gloria. But she was busy placing a lace cloth on a low table and fussing with it. She added some unusual objects to the table – her dressmaking scissors, a square of silk, a red towel, white candles, a bar of Cadbury's chocolate and a jug of water.

'Ammi, what sort of a party —' I started to say when the door opened and Meher Aunty waddled in. She took a key out of her pocket and turned it in the door. I hadn't even known the door could be locked. I really wanted this to be my room.

'Ah, good, it's all set up,' Meher said, a wheeze rattling her breath. 'Is she clean?'

'Of course she is.' The Magician drew me close again and kissed the top of my head, her touch hesitant and her voice ragged. 'You've just had a bath, haven't you, Maryam? Washed your hair?'

I nodded, an uneasy knocking starting in my chest, especially when the Magician looked away and drew a deep breath.

Meher looked at me suspiciously and picked up the scissors, clicking them open to peer at the blades before reaching into her pocket for another, smaller pair. 'Okay,' she said, 'better jump up on the table. Take your knickers off first. It won't take long. Farah, you stand on this side, away from the light.'

The question I was about to ask was stopped by a thump on the closed door. Meher and the Magician put a finger to their lips and shook their heads slowly. I shut my mouth and stayed still.

The thump became a rapid knocking and Gloria's high voice filtered through. 'Ammi? Are you in there? Open the door, Ammi. Hannah? Are you there too?'

The Magician clutched me too tightly and Meher clamped a sweaty fist around my arm. They set their faces and held me as if I would run away.

'Open the door, Hannah. For God's sake, open the door. Ammi! I'm going to keep knocking and shouting till you open this door. Mrs D'Silva will hear me shouting and I'll tell her everything. I mean it. You will open this door or...or...' Gloria's voice was louder now and the Magician flinched. I stopped struggling in her grip. Meher took her hand away to wipe her face. I twisted free and ran to the door.

'They've got a key, Gloria. It's locked from the inside. They're both here. Ammi and her. Gloria, what can I do? I'm scared. Please don't go. Please don't shout. What's the matter? Help me, Gloria. Call someone.' I pounded on the door and Gloria continued thumping on it from the outside.

'Hannah.'

'Maryam.'

'Such headstrong girls you have.'

'I shouldn't have listened to you. This is not our custom. We don't do this to our girls. I am Iranian.'

'You are nothing. Your people came here as refugees. You forget.'

'They are your people too, Meher. This is not an Iranian custom. Please.'

'Farah, have you forgotten Rani? How much better it would have been? Hot country like this, hot blood in their veins – it's for their own good.'

Meher and the Magician kept their voices low but I heard every word as I hit my palm on the door behind which my sister was shouting.

'Maryam, shush, please, my darling, here…' the Magician came up behind me and handed me the key. She didn't look at me.

I pulled the door open and Gloria fell into the room. 'Hannah, are you okay? They haven't done it yet? Oh, I should have warned you.'

'Done what? Ammi said it was going to be a secret party – like the one you had. I thought I was getting new clothes. Ammi, you said it was a party.'

'Yes, Ammi. Why don't you tell her what she's getting?' Gloria's voice choked with tears.

She never cried, not even when the Historian rampaged through the house in one of his moods, telling us what he would do if he caught us. I was the crybaby. And Gloria put her hands over my ears and cradled me gently, and I knew she wouldn't ever let the Historian catch me. But now her tears fell down her cheeks and onto our linked hands. The Magician looked as if she might cry too, and Meher clucked like an angry hen.

Gloria dragged me out of the room and into the garden. She looked around quickly. It was afternoon and no one was outside. We ran past the courtyard, out the main gates and into the ragged street that led to the markets. They weren't open today – it was the saint's special day and all the shopkeepers had gone to the shrine to show respect. We heard them chant as they walked past, carrying their orange flags and flowers. The square around the banyan tree was empty, so we climbed up and sat on the cracked concrete. Dust swirled around our feet, and a couple of bearded goats walked hopefully towards us.

Gloria let go of my hand. She wiped her face with her palms and drew deep breaths. 'You know your little thing down there, Hannah? It's called a clitoris. The little thing you're not supposed to touch or play with?'

What was she saying? We didn't talk about things like that. The aunties said it was *chee chee*. They said we shouldn't touch it or look at it. They said it would get us into all sorts of trouble when we grew up. One little cut would fix us, they said. No one had explained what that meant. Until now.

Gloria's voice was still croaky with tears. 'No one is allowed to touch it. Remember that, Hannah. No one. Not the Magician. Not Meher Aunty. Don't let anyone near it. Don't ever take your knickers off and lie down on that table. They – they were going to cut you there. Those scissors were going to cut off your clitoris and the chocolate was supposed to make you feel better. It doesn't.'

I looked at Gloria. Tears drenched her face again. She let them fall. I reached out and wiped her face gently, rubbing her tears away with my hands. 'Why?' I asked. 'Why would they do that?'

'Because we're girls, that's why.'

'I don't understand. Is it like a punishment? Did we do something wrong?'

'Yes. We were born girls and that's wrong. Mind you, they do it to boys too, but properly, in a hospital, with doctors and anaesthetics and everything. Bet it doesn't hurt them as much as it hurts us. It hurts *us* a lot.'

'Did they do it to you, Gloria?'

'Yes. In that room. That's why I don't go there. I'm sorry I lied to you about the *djinns*. There aren't any *djinns* but you were too young to understand. I said I wouldn't let it happen to you. I thought they'd wait until you were older – you know, at least till you were twelve. That's when they did me. It's not the Magician's fault. She cried as much as I did afterwards. She said she was sorry.' Gloria spoke in her normal voice now and I breathed in, watching her face.

'I know. It's that horrible Meher Aunty.'

'I really wish she would die.'

'When I grow up, I'll poison her. I'll get arsenic, like they do in the Agatha Christie books.'

'Hannah, I'll always look after you. I can't believe how close you came to...'

We held each other in the shade of the banyan tree, our hands sticky with tears and sweat. A couple of boys from the village rode up on their bicycles and whistled when the wind flicked our dresses up around our legs.

'Oy, sweetie,' they said loudly, and sang a Hindi film song, thrusting their hips at us.

Gloria jumped down from the square and shouted, 'Get lost or I'll send my father after you with a gun, you dogs,' and the boys wheeled away, still whistling and sneering.

Twenty-one

'Move in with me, Hannah,' Gabriel said abruptly one afternoon when we stood on the verandah of his cottage, looking down at the city.

Perth was wrapped in haze. Bushfires had recently swept through the hills, and we knew people had lost their homes barely ten kilometres from where we stood. A peppery smell of ash hung in the afternoon heat. Gabriel volunteered at the Fire and Rescue Service. He'd been out all morning and had come back weary and grim, muttering about the little sod who had deliberately started one of several fires in the state forest.

'What?' I breathed in too sharply and sneezed.

'You heard me,' Gabriel said and offered me a crumpled hanky.

'I can't do that,' I said, shaking my head at the sight of the untidy ball he held out towards me.

'Why not? Aren't I the best thing since sliced bread? Don't you adore me?'

'For a minute there I thought you were serious.' I laughed and tucked my arm through his. 'I practically live here, anyway.'

'I am serious.' Gabriel turned me around to face him, eyes unreadable, forehead wrinkling, heartbeat loud under the palm I placed on his chest. He was like a primal memory – I remembered him in a way that didn't make sense.

'Let me think about it,' I said. There were too many things he didn't know.

'That I won't.' The laughter was back in his eyes, his hands warm on my body, his kiss confident on my mouth.

He smelled of smoke and charred wood and I loved him.

The cottage wall shielded us from the sun and the city continued to simmer below us. Ivy and star jasmine clung to walls and shaded the pathways to Gabriel's garden. 'Clever companion planting,' he had said when I first admired this abundant garden, a solitary spot of green among the brown lawns and straggly gum trees that surrounded us. With an arm around my waist he pointed out the layers and colours. 'You put all the drought-resistant natives along the edge – see? Put the fussy ones underneath. Herbs and vegies in boxes, so you can keep an eye on them. Chuck in some stinking geraniums to confuse the bugs, and Bob's your uncle. I hate lawns. Don't see the point of them, especially in a climate like ours. A hangover from old England, I suppose, this obsession with having a lawn out the front. I ripped out all the grass when I bought the place. You know much about gardening, Hannah?'

'Not that much,' I'd said, thinking about the Magician's garden and how she planted in different seasons but scattered coriander seeds everywhere, all the time. We could never have enough coriander. She only used the leaves and threw away the stalks, where all the flavour was. I would have a herb garden, I decided, a proper herb garden, if I lived here with Gabriel. Not rosemary and parsley. I would grow coriander and green chilli and sweet basil and curry leaf and bay leaf and fennel and a frangipani – a cream frangipani. Maybe some nasturtiums.

The cottage had belonged to an old man whose junk still lived in the tin shed at the back of the house. For several years after he sold the cottage to Gabriel, old Bill used to come and potter around in the shed, pointing out the history behind each item, regretting he had run out of time to do something with them. Long planks of thick wood, handsaws hanging from hooks, jam jars filled with screws and nails, tins that couldn't be opened because rust had sealed them shut – it was Aladdin's cave without the genie lamp.

Gabriel raised his eyebrows when I offered to tidy up. 'You mean you want to throw this stuff out, don't you?'

'No,' I said. 'We can sort it into categories – good junk, bad junk. Bad junk can be put out on the verge. To make room for other things – like gardening tools and compost bins.'

'No such thing as bad junk. There's a man's life here – in boxes and unfinished tables and brass handles and old ledgers with scrawly handwriting. It would be sacrilege to throw it out.'

'For someone who hasn't spoken to his siblings in ten years and is vague about his mother's current address, you're very sentimental about an old man's rusty boxes,' I said.

'But will you look at them? The rusty boxes have brass latches. Who makes square tin boxes with latches these days?'

I remembered a square tin box of my own, given to me by a captive aunt. 'Promise me you'll never look inside,' she'd said, and I had obeyed.

'Tell me about your dad, Gabriel,' I said.

'I guess he decided he didn't want to live any more,' Gabriel said, squeezing my hand. 'He was a rough old codger, but he wasn't mean. I didn't see much of him. He left my mum when I was twelve and I left home when I was sixteen, so it wasn't like he was a big part of my life. He was living in Hobart when he topped himself.'

I let his arm circle my waist before I spoke. 'I wonder what my life would have been like if my father had disappeared instead of my mother.'

'We'd be sitting here comparing notes on whether it's better to have a dead dad or an absconding one. Come on, misery guts, let's go and cook something – or better still, let's tidy up the shed. Can't have you moping around if you're going to live here. In this house there are rules – and rule number one is you're not allowed to be miserable.'

'I didn't say — '

'You will.'

I followed him through the house and into the back where his red kelpie, Jarrah, lay panting under the casuarina. She lifted wet eyes and whined, tail thumping as Gabriel bent down and scratched her ears. She turned on her back with a low growl, stretched and yawned. 'See, she's ignoring you now,' Gabriel said. 'Told you she was a sook. She's used to being the only girl in my life, that's all.'

I edged past her, keeping Gabriel in front of me, just in case. Jarrah had fastened her teeth on my arm when I first met her. She had growled and dribbled, and Gabriel put his hand on her collar and talked to her quietly, firmly, till she let my arm go. He was gentle with both of us – he gave me lemonade with a shot of brandy as he rubbed aloe vera on the bruise forming on my arm, then went outside and knelt beside the dog as she sat on the steps with flattened ears and downcast tail.

Afterwards he held me against his chest and stroked my hair and murmured apologies. 'It's my fault,' he said, voice deep with remorse. 'I'll keep her on a lead till she gets used to you.'

At the door to the shed, I stopped Gabriel by placing my hand in his. 'Okay,' I said. 'I'll move in with you. And I'll have that mutt eating out of my hand by the weekend.'

Twenty-two

As with most things he did, the Historian announced his decision to take my brothers and me to Australia without any warning. I had been so busy keeping a vigil for the ones who had gone that at first the announcement didn't register. It interfered with my count of days without them. The Magician (and Rani) had been gone for one hundred and eighty-two days, Gloria seventy-four days, Sohrab sixty-seven days and Meher sixty-five days. I turned fourteen and no one noticed.

The only departure I rejoiced in was Meher's. She hadn't gone empty-handed. She filled bag after bag with things from the house – bedsheets, shawls, quilts, curtains, cutlery, plates and tea sets – and the Historian hadn't stopped her. She had said that word in my ear before she left. '*Harami*,' she had said. 'Bastard.'

The Historian was in the library on the day the removalists came. Most of the books had been taken from the shelves and put in large wooden crates. Grandpa Billy's diaries and the conquistadors remained where they'd always been – occupying the top two shelves.

'Aren't you going to pack those?' I pointed at the blue-and-gold books.

'What for?' the Historian asked, brows furrowing. 'I don't want to carry the old man's rubbish across the oceans and into our new lives. They're falling to bits – probably have silverfish. Australians are very strict about germs and what we are allowed to bring into the country. None of the slack-twisted ways of this blighted country will work there, Hannah, and you better remember this. I'm throwing these books out. Should have burned them with the rest.'

'I like those books.'

'I'll buy you better ones when we get to Australia.'

'I don't want to go to Australia.'

'Don't be ridiculous.'

Clive and Warren were no comfort. They tried to be practical. 'Oh, come on, Hannah,' they said. 'Most girls your age haven't even been to Bombay and you're going to Perth. Surely that's a little bit exciting? It's going to be a better life, you know – like going abroad to study, except we're going abroad to live.'

'But don't you see? How will the Magician and Gloria ever find us if we leave? It's not like the Historian ever spoke of Australia when we all lived together. They won't know where we are, but if we stay here – there's a chance they'll come.'

Clive hugged me absently and Warren turned his face away. They didn't remind me of the part I had played in one of those departures.

I looked around the home I was about to lose. This archaic bungalow with high ceilings and secret rooms held our lives in its confines. This house where the aunties and cousins slept in the afternoons and we plotted their downfall – these rooms where we heard voices and whispers – this was the only home I'd ever known. My English grandfather had passed it down to his son, and the Historian told us Clive would inherit it and his son after him. The gaolhouse windows, once transformed by sari curtains, were stark against the grey sky. The tomb-like beds used to have *khadi* bedspreads and mirror-work cushions. Now all that remained of the Magician were empty vases and scrunched-up *sofrehs*. The house was already hollow with absence.

The Historian had relatives in Australia. So disinclined was he to own up to his family that we had always assumed Rani was his only living relative. And he had locked her up until the Magician set her free. Now, he told us he had a cousin and we had second cousins, girls my age, whom I would meet for the first time in Australia. I would go to their school; they would help me settle in.

'My cousin Francine is a remarkable woman,' the Historian said to us on our last night in Devnagri. Our possessions were boxed and already on their way. All my clothes and books were crammed into two new suitcases with wheels. 'She has two girls of her own and she has fostered several unfortunate children who had nowhere to go. It's amazing that a prosperous country like Australia also has this problem of homeless children. But, unlike in this godforsaken place, there people like Frankie have a social conscience. And they help out.'

'We helped out,' I mumbled. 'We took in people who had nowhere else to go. Don't you remember? You were always complaining.'

'Are you being cheeky, girl? Are you defying me?' The Historian's eyes blinked quickly and his cheeks started their slow splash of red. Clive took my arm and urged me out the door.

'Hannah, please don't make trouble now – we've got too much to do. Why must you talk to him at all? You go for days without noticing he's there and at exactly the worst time you decide to say something? I can't always be here to watch out for you.' Clive shook me and I twisted out of his grip.

'Am I the only one who can see he's taking us to live with some woman who sounds like the Magician?'

'Hannah, for God's sake – she's his cousin.'

'So he says.'

I wondered if I would be able to persuade my brothers to carry the rest of the conquistador books. I had sneaked in all my favourites,

Clive and Warren Hastings and Lord Louie, but was torn between Dalhousie and Bentinck. I preferred Dalhousie because he had a town named after him that we had once visited. I didn't remember being there but the Magician had spoken of it with a faraway look in her eyes. 'I had never seen snow before, Maryam, and the whole place was covered in snow – just like a fairytale – and you were happy too. You liked the snow. Every time I carried you to the window you went quiet, and I knew you were looking at the snow. You were so tiny and the snow was so thick. Yes, it was a special place – for a special child. You and I were alone for the first time,' the Magician stroked my cheek and pulled me onto her lap, rocking me as if I were a baby again.

'Was it just us, Ammi? No one else?'

'Uh-huh. I think so. I don't remember anyone else. Why would I, when you were so beautiful and I had eyes only for you?'

'Hannah? Are you listening?' The Historian stared at me over the table. His knuckles tapped the table and the hand formed a fist. My heart lurched. 'I'm talking to you. You're not sulking because of the books, are you?'

'Of course not,' I said, avoiding his eyes and clattering away from the table. 'Can I go to bed now?'

Dalhousie was going to Australia with me. Under his *rigorous* administration, India had entered an era of material and social progress. And because he was part of the memory the Magician had made with me.

It rained all night. I lay on the stripped bed and listened to sounds I would never hear again. The wind whistled through gaps and large raindrops splattered first on the roof before hurling themselves at the windows. Monsoons always began savagely here. The bald hills offered no protection against rain-choked winds, and the house groaned like an old man with a heavy load on his back. Streams of muddy water collected behind the house, sloshing outside my window. In the morning, the gardener would divert it away from the house and fill up the damp hollows with stones. With the next downpour, the same thing would happen; the stones would be washed away and refilled. When we were children, Clive made paper boats and helped me float them, and the Magician fried samosas and made carrot halva. Then she sent me up the stairs to check on Rani. The attic was susceptible to damp and rot.

I lay there as my brother walked past my room and went to the bathroom. The door scrunched where it dragged on the concrete. Clive turned on the water at the sink, washed his face and splashed water on the floor. He left the light on for Warren and walked past again, tapping twice on my door as he did. 'Good night,' I called out. I thought about Gloria and Sohrab and the Magician and the time we had all lived here – in this house, this man-house. The ghosts of the aunties clattered past and Meher's voice cackled abuse.

I knew very little about Australia. Mrs D'Silva told me I would have a nice time there, as if I were going on a picnic with her daughters when they came to visit from their city schools. One of Gloria's discarded Mills & Boon novels had Australian characters – laconic, hardy men who strummed guitars and said 'mate' and 'onya'. Olivia Newton-John was Australian, and Perth was the windiest city in the world after Chicago, according to the Historian. Three things, three unrelated things – snippets from a romance novel, pop music and the Historian's lofty statement – were all I knew about the country he was determined to call home.

'As a business migrant, I didn't have to go through all the usual rubbish of finding a sponsor and all that.' The Historian settled into the seat beside me and patted the pockets on his new suit. I looked back at him and he raised an eyebrow.

'Okay, tell me more,' I said from my spot between him and Clive. Warren had the aisle seat in front of us and had already pushed it back as far as it would go, grinning when the Historian tapped him and asked him to straighten up. Clive leaned back and closed his eyes.

The Historian pulled out a photograph of a woman and two girls standing outside a red-brick house with striped awnings and a patch of grass struggling beside the slope of a steep driveway. 'Your Aunty Frankie and her girls. It'll be all right, I promise. You'll have a good life now – in this country – far away from those superstitious women and dusty old books. This is a young country, a happy place – it'll be all right.'

I can never have a good life with you, I thought. *You are the reason I am alone.* 'Sounds all right, Dad,' I said and turned my face away. I now knew a fourth thing about Australia. A corrupt ex-policeman masquerading as a business migrant was acceptable in this 'wide brown land'.

Twenty-three

My first sight of a white beach fringing a blue ocean in Perth rendered me speechless. Nothing could have prepared me for that ostentatious sky, silver sand and emerald water on a summer morning. It looked like the empty set of a Hollywood movie, waves swishing gently towards the shore and cast waiting unseen. And the light. It was different. It was too much. All that light pouring from the sky and rising up from the sea and filling the beach. A blue sky with clouds sketched over it, white sand that lay on the shoreline and an ocean without a boat or human being in sight. Empty, except for the light – the light was a presence, a tangible presence. I turned to my Australian cousin, Sally, whose eyes were shielded by white-framed sunglasses.

'Pretty, isn't it?' Sally said, linking her arm through mine. 'Still gets me every time – and I was born here. We always bring visitors to this spot. Love their reaction.'

I took off my shoes and the sand claimed my feet. Cold and dry. I curled my toes into it. 'I didn't know sand could feel so lovely,' I said and Sally grinned.

'Where are all the people?' I bent down and picked up a handful of that white sand and let it trickle through my fingers. I wanted to taste it. To see if it really was sand.

'Down at Scarborough, I expect. That's where all the surfies go. There's too much seaweed here, and they don't like it. Suits us – our private beach. Who needs a pool when you have this in your backyard? Wanna swim, Hannah? Did you bring your bathers?' Sally untied her sarong and ran into the water, bouncing up and down in her green bikini. When I finally made it to the water's edge, it was cold and I stood there with the Indian Ocean slapping my ankles until I got used to it.

Maybe it was teenage resilience, maybe it was being in a city so clean, so unlike the dry, dusty bustle of Devnagri, that misery wasn't an option. Perth had a freshly scrubbed look about it – a clean, swept look. A long road with scarlet roses dividing it at the centre led up to Kings Park, where tall eucalypts carried the names of lost soldiers at their base and the hill sloped down towards the city and the river. The Historian stood for several minutes staring at the War Memorial while my brothers and I walked towards the lookout where tourists took photos of the pretty city below them. People didn't run to catch buses or shove to get in front of you. There were never any queues. Cars didn't toot their horns unless the driver was upset or saying goodbye. Everyone said thank you ('Ta') and asked if you were all right ('You right?').

The Historian's cousin was a friendly, practical woman who tossed us into her busy life and expected us to pitch in. Aunty Frankie was used to having a large, unwieldy household, and like the Magician made sure there was plenty of food for everyone. Huge quantities of bread, pasta, mince, potatoes and iceberg lettuce were rotated on a nightly basis. Uncle Steve was a geologist who worked up north and only came home for six weeks in the year. Aunty Frankie said they were saving to buy a bigger house and set themselves up for life. They called the Historian 'Gordy' and seemed to think he was 'cool'.

The girls, my new cousins, looked after me at school. 'We're mates,' Sally said cheerfully, and her younger sister Lisa blew me a kiss. They shared their clothes with me and took me shopping on Thursday nights.

'Your dad's loaded,' Lisa said with a wink. 'Hit him for a couple of fifties, why don't you? And you can get some really cool stuff, coz, no offence, but your Indian clothes are a bit daggy.'

I looked at my handloom kurta and blue jeans (chosen in memory of a sister who had left a large black hole in my heart) and was instantly ashamed. Sally thumped Lisa and said, 'Ignore the pest. Your clothes are cool. You wear what you like. We're laid-back here. No one cares.'

Aunty Frankie and her girls helped us move into the Historian's house. She wasn't especially thrilled that he had chosen to live miles away from anywhere, but I could have told her why. The big stone house, surrounded by paddocks and vineyards and purple trees, was far enough away from the only family we had in a brand-new country. If the Historian decided to lock up an errant daughter, no one would know. Aunty Frankie wasn't sure it was a good investment – too far from the city even if it had a nice view.

'Still, far be it for me to comment,' Aunty Frankie said with a raised eyebrow. 'I suppose you know what you want – and you can always sell it if you change your mind after a couple of years. It's hard to know what suits you at first. Not to worry – lots of places around, I can tell you.'

'I'm buying land, Frankie. The house just happens to be on it. Two acres of prime land that will definitely go up in value, you'll see. I'll develop it. I can put six houses on it. I've been speaking to estate agents who know these things. Proximity to the city is not the only criterion. You need to be far-sighted and make a long-term investment.' The Historian waved his arm around and bared his teeth.

Aunty Frankie smiled and called him a 'dodgy old bugger'.

The kitchen was stocked first. Shelves in the pantry were filled with flour, rice, beans, pasta, sugar and cans of tuna, corn and tomatoes. The Magician would have approved (and added almonds, saffron, fennel, orange oil).

'Don't worry, Hannah,' Aunty Frankie said when I switched on the kettle and looked around for tea. She pulled tea bags out of a square yellow box. 'The boys are going to help. Aren't you?' She called out to my brothers. 'This isn't India. Everyone needs to pull their weight. And until you settle down, the girls and I will bring some meals around. Go on, love, take a load off. I'll make you a cuppa.'

I moved a tattered cookbook titled *Budget Meals for Australians* out of the way before leaning my elbows on the benchtop. I knew the names of all the Magician's herbs, fresh and dried. I had helped Sohrab label those herbs. He wrote crookedly and capitalised randomly. The labels had remained on the empty bottles till the day we left. I had no idea what to do with parsley and rosemary.

'Where can I get some cumin, coriander and turmeric, Aunty Frankie?' I asked.

'No idea, love. I'll see if I can get them from the Asian shop in Northbridge. You better write those names down for me – and anything else you think of. Actually, I have a better idea. You come with me and we can buy them together, eh?'

The Asian shop in Northbridge smelled like the Magician's kitchen. I bought five kinds of dal and basmati rice as well as cumin, coriander, turmeric, chilli and salt. Aunty Frankie exclaimed over my purchases and asked what I was going to do with them. 'When I make curry, I just use Clive of India. I like it hot, you see, but the kids complain,' she said cheerfully, adding a small tin with the words Clive of India above the picture of a conquistador.

'He was a common thug, you know,' I said. 'Clive of India was a robber. He stole our country and handed it over to the British. I read about him when I was little.'

'What an intense little thing you are, Hannah. You mustn't take things so seriously, love. It's just a brand name. But I'll put it back if you feel so strongly.'

I was quiet, thinking I'd offended her. At home I filled little plastic bottles with herbs and larger plastic bottles with dal and rice and labelled them all. Then I stood back and looked at them. How did the Magician transform this into food it still hurts to remember? Ammi.

Twenty-four

The Historian evicted Sohrab from the house despite our efforts to calm him down and make him see some sense. Mrs D'Silva took Sohrab in and Gloria stopped speaking to me. I didn't get it. Why was Gloria so angry? Sohrab moving next door gave them more freedom. They should thank me instead of looking at me as if I'd ripped their hearts out. He had his own room at the back of the house and Gloria didn't have to go through the main house to be with him. My brothers, too, spent more time next door. The Historian and Meher bickered about my sister and mother.

'*Toba*,' Meher said. 'This is what happens when you start breeding children like animals. I warned your unfortunate wife this would happen. Such behaviour – even animals have more self-control than that daughter of yours.'

'I'll break both his legs,' the Historian said. 'I'll put his eyes out. He thinks he can defile my family. I'll show him. I'll break his arms. Then I'll cut off his balls.'

'Not content with little half-breeds running around all day, you had to go and add a *firangi* to the mix. What did you expect? Low-class peasants – all of you,' Meher said.

'Oh, shut up, old woman,' the Historian said. 'Why are you still here? Haven't you done enough damage? This is your fault – filling Farah's ears with nonsense. I should shoot you down with my revolver.'

'Just you try it, mister. My son is a lawyer and I have witnesses.'

'You really think threatening me with a two-paisa lawyer is going to scare me?'

'*Badmash*,' said Meher. 'You forget I know everything.'

The Historian's eyes fixed on her. 'You forget I own you *and* your family.'

The Historian said he would make us all pay. He described what he would do with Sohrab after he broke his legs (and cut off his balls). He wiped his revolver with a yellow cloth and aimed it at the door of the room I used to share with Gloria. Clive and Warren shielded me with their bodies when I screamed, and the Historian said I was hysterical and should be locked up in Rani's empty room. He muttered the Magician's name in the evenings when he sat with a glass of scotch and a deep furrow between his brows. Sometimes he said '*Kamini saali churail*' quickly and viciously, and I prayed he would never find my mother and aunt. At least Gloria was safe with the D'Silvas. I was too angry with Sohrab to care about the state of his limbs if the Historian made good his threat.

I begged the night servant to take me to her house and she said she would stay with me all night, rolling out a mattress beside my bed and telling me stories about the brothers who lived in the cave on the hills until I fell asleep. In the morning she was gone. I thought about running away. I picked up all the loose change in the house and went through my brothers' pockets when their pants were hanging up behind the door. Raids on the Historian's pockets were far more lucrative. By the end of the week I had fifty rupees.

'Why aren't you at school, Hannah?' The Historian looked up from the morning paper, removed his reading glasses and pointed at the time on the grandfather clock.

'I'm not going to school. Everyone's laughing at us.'

'You're too sensitive. Just ignore them. It's not for long anyway.'

What did he mean?

'Summer holidays are coming up. You'll have plenty of time to play then. Now, go to school. And if anyone bothers you, tell me their name,' the Historian said, putting his glasses back on and picking up the newspaper.

I spent the morning walking around the gardens of the municipal offices down the road from our house. Too many people used the gardens as a thoroughfare to worry about a schoolgirl sitting on a bench with a green journal open on her lap, looking as if she was doing her homework. If I looked up and made eye contact, I got a nod and a friendly smile. It was good to have something to do, somewhere to go, away from the house.

I did this every morning, dreading the weekend. Weekdays were now peaceful. I sat on my bench and studied the Magician's journals. Sometimes I cried. I didn't know where I could run away to. I wanted Gloria to talk to me again. I wished my brothers wouldn't ignore me.

'Maryam.' The voice was soft and familiar. It was lunchtime and I was about to go to the cigarette shop to buy some lollies with my secret stash of cash. I looked at Sohrab's feet in the dirt near the bench where I sat. The wide limbs of the banyan tree shaded this spot and gave off a dry smell. 'Can I sit with you?'

'I'm sorry, Sohrab. I'm so sorry. I'm a wicked girl. I should never —'

'Please, Maryam. It is my fault. You are too young and you don't know – I have watched you every day and I know you don't go to school. Everything is going wrong.'

I sobbed and he made low clicking sounds but didn't touch me, not even when I sidled along the bench and grabbed his hand. His breathing slowed and his back went rigid. I put my head on his shoulder and leaned against him.

'I miss you all so much,' I said. 'I miss Gloria. Please make her talk to me again.'

Sohrab moved my head away from his shoulder but let me hold his hand. 'You are all stubborn – stubborn women – and everything is all wrong and I have no money for anything.'

'Here,' I said, reaching into my bag and pulling out the crushed notes and loose change tied in the Magician's embroidered hanky. 'I was going to use this to run away, but I don't know where to run to. You can have it. You probably need it for cigarettes and —'

'I feel too bad, Maryam, but thank you. I will take it. I have only two rupees left. Can you get me some more? This will be enough for a week. I can meet you here again next week?'

'Yes, yes. I can get you more. I'll really get you some more. Please, can you bring Gloria next time? Please make her talk to me?'

Sohrab took off his glasses and polished them. He nodded and looked away.

Twenty-five

Acquiring an Australian accent was easy. As long as I populated my speech with the same words other teens used, I fitted in. I stretched out my vowels and learned to be monosyllabic. I didn't finish my sentences, sulked when asked to do something, skipped homework and smoked with my cousins in the backyard. My Australian school was nothing like my Indian school. The nuns here looked like everyone else. They didn't wear starched white habits and threaten us with black spots on our souls or punish us with sweeping the yard if we talked in class. Schoolwork was easy. I didn't let slip how much I knew. Watching TV helped my accent and vocabulary – the Channel Seven News ('Love you, Perth'), and *Neighbours* ('*Everybody needs good neighbours*').

My cousins took me to the movies on occasional Tuesdays and we hung around the shops afterwards, trying on clothes and giggling at grown-ups. I learned to say 'arvo' and 'too easy' and 'See ya later, alligator'.

'You right there, Hannah?' Aunty Frankie asked one Thursday evening when I pushed my food around the plate, wondering if I would be allowed to spend the weekend with them. The Historian frowned at me from the other side of the table. My brothers had come for dinner, and then disappeared quickly with their girlfriends.

'Yes, thanks. Want me to finish up here?'

'Knock yourself out. I've got a foster-parents meeting tomorrow.'

'Hey, Mum, can Sal and me and Hannah chuck a sickie tomorrow? Please, please? School really sucks and we haven't had a sickie all term.'

I knew why Lisa was petitioning her mother to let us all have the day off. She was in *lurve* and wanted to sneak off with her tattooed mechanic boyfriend. Sally couldn't stand him and I wasn't a big fan either, but we were mates and sisters so we said nothing. The Historian said he didn't mind if I had the day off.

'All right,' Aunty Frankie said distractedly, 'but I expect some chores done. You can't lie around being princesses all day.'

'Aw, thanks, Mum, Uncle Gordy, you're the best.' Lisa grinned at us and Sally scowled. I kept my face neutral, resigned to dragging myself around the shops after them.

'She's such a skank sometimes,' Sally said at the shops while Lisa and Luke held hands and he rubbed her bottom. 'I mean, seriously, why would you let *that* put his hands all over you? Spew.'

'No accounting for taste,' I agreed, thinking of another pair of lovers holding hands near a turtle pond years ago. Unlike these two, Sohrab and Gloria didn't want to be seen, did not ask for what happened next.

Twenty-six

'What are you doing with the money?' Clive asked quietly one evening as he followed me to my room. I hadn't seen Warren for two nights and usually Clive went to his own room after dinner instead of seeking me out. I had become a bold, possibly careless thief. When the Historian gave me money for a new uniform and books, I didn't give him back any change and asked for more the following week. I was also stealing food money and the servants had been in trouble twice. A quick glance sideways and I knew there wasn't any point in stalling.

'I'm giving it to Sohrab. He hasn't got any and he wants to go back to Iran. He has to pay board and his tuition fees.'

'How much have you given him?'

'I don't know. Maybe two or three hundred rupees. Please don't be angry. I just wanted to help them.'

'Them?'

'Yes, he's looking after Gloria. He said he was.'

Clive sighed and put an arm around me. 'You need to stop this, Hannah. Three hundred rupees isn't going to get Sohrab to Iran. He has a return ticket. He can go any time he wants. He doesn't pay board. Come with me. I need to show you something.'

Alarm knocked against my chest as I followed Clive to Mrs D'Silva's house. I had not been inside since Sohrab's eviction three months ago. The old couple were in the front room by a small window and looked up as we entered.

'Hannah, my girl. We don't see you any more. We miss you.' Mrs D'Silva smelled of Yardley talc and candied ginger. I stepped into her outstretched arms and kissed her cheek.

'Clive? What were you going to show me?' I whispered when Mrs D'Silva clattered off into the kitchen and Mr D'Silva slumped in the chair with his eyes closed.

'You'll see.' Clive was grim.

We sat in the gloom with a plate of stale cupcakes in front of us and pretended to eat them. Mr D'Silva snored in his chair and Mrs D'Silva knitted a round cap-like thing in blue wool. A radio crackled beside her and she chatted to us intermittently. I wondered where Gloria was. Already in bed? Did they share a room?

The front door opened with a squeak and a column of light from the street fell briefly across the hallway. Two silhouettes appeared in the yellow light and Mrs D'Silva tapped her husband awake. The shadows of Warren and Sohrab took their shoes off at the door and tiptoed across the room, not seeing us at first. Mrs D'Silva said loudly, 'We are going to bed now. You children stay as long as you like. Sohrab will lock up after you. Won't you, my son?'

Clive kissed her goodnight. She hurried her husband out of the room and Warren lurched towards us. He flung his arms around me, smelling of booze, cigarettes and sweat. 'Good to see you, sweetie,' he said, and Clive steadied him as I slipped out of the embrace. Sohrab helped lower Warren into the chair vacated by Mr D'Silva. We sat down as before and Clive switched on the table lamp. Sohrab's face was as flushed as Warren's, and he smiled at me in a silly, blind way that made me want to punch him.

'You see this, Hannah?' Clive sounded like the Historian. 'This is what you've been stealing for. This fellow' – he pointed at Sohrab – 'and your brother, out drinking most nights, thanks to you. You don't even know where Gloria is, do you?'

'Where is she?' I kept my voice low. 'Clive, don't be like this. What's going on?'

'Maryam,' said Sohrab, 'it is good you are here.'

'Don't call me that, you…you liar. Don't use my mother's name for me – ever.'

'Gloria's in Bombay. She's living with Mrs D'Silva's daughter.' Clive's words fell in the room like dust and I didn't believe him. Gloria might be angry with me but she wouldn't leave without telling me. She'd never do what the Magician had done.

'Broke my heart,' said Sohrab, punching a fist to his chest. 'I was going to marry her. She broke my heart. Now I have nothing. No country, no wife. And all because of this *shaitoon*…' he pointed towards Warren.

Warren flung his head back and snored.

'Come on, Hannah.' Clive bent down and shook Warren. 'Help me get him home. Sohrab, go to bed and don't wake the old people.' I picked up Warren's shoes at the door and looked back at Sohrab sitting on the chair with a hand splayed across his chest.

'She didn't say goodbye. Does she hate me that much?' I offered my arm to support Warren, and Clive sighed.

'She doesn't hate you. She needs some time on her own, that's all. She'll come back when she's figured it out. She doesn't hate you.'

'And Sohrab?'

'Sohrab is not your problem. Let's try and figure out how we're going to get Warren into his room without the Historian finding us first.'

In his room, Warren stretched his lanky frame, holding out his arms to allow us to undress him and get him to bed. 'Dish my fault,' he said slowly, looking up at me. 'Dish my fault Gloria ran away. Hannah, don't run away.' He turned over on his stomach and started snoring.

'Don't,' Clive said when I turned to him. 'Don't ask another question. I'm sick of this. You all need to grow up and face facts. Your mother isn't here to pick up after you any more, and who knows what your father is going to do when he finds out.'

Mrs D'Silva came to our house at ten the next morning. 'He's gone,' she said, her voice shaking. 'Sohrab's gone. Poor little fellow. His things are gone – room empty – must have left in the night. Where will he go? What will he do? He's not well. He has no money, no family.'

'Good riddance,' the Historian said. 'We don't want fundamentalist Muslims around, especially foreigners. It's okay, Aunty Jean, he's got plenty of money. Our Hannah gave him some.'

Twenty-seven

I moved in with Gabriel on a weekend in April, the year I turned twenty-five. I had been working as a research assistant in the State Library for a year. I had a car, a rough-looking yellow Corolla with a top speed of eighty kilometres on the freeway. By Australian standards I was an independent young woman with a steady boyfriend and a great job. By Indian standards I was an immoral young woman living in sin with a foreigner.

The Anzac Day public holiday meant my brothers and their girlfriends were around to help. I didn't have any furniture except the bookcase Gabriel had made for me when I lived with Anya. My brothers grumbled and stuffed my clothes and books and shoes into plastic bags, muttering about my junk. Gabriel told them to 'Stop being such girls' and get on with it, organising our clumsy efforts to pack the cars and going back inside the house for a final look before making the trip to his cottage in the hills.

Jarrah thumped her tail but didn't move from her vigil on the verandah as we emptied cars and placed boxes in a corner of the family room. I walked past her carefully, gaining confidence when she ignored me.

∞

Afterwards, in the quickening chill of early winter, we made coffee and sat on the verandah with an open packet of Tim Tams resting on my lap. The garden smelled of crushed peppermint and chocolate. White cockatoos flew past the marri trees, their calls fading as they disappeared over the crest of the hill. The sky glowed briefly before plunging us into a moonless night. Silence then, except for the crickets, cicadas and butcherbirds.

'Gidgegannup,' I said, tapping Gabriel on his knee.

'What?'

'I used to play word games with Gloria when we were little. Australian place names are so musical – you know, like Gidgegannup and Bidyadanga and Bundoora.'

'Woolloomooloo,' said Gabriel, grinning.

'Indooroopilly.'

'Yackandandah, Badgingarra, Mandjoogoordap. I can go on all night, Hannah. I've lived here longer than you.'

Gabriel reached his hand out towards the dog and whistled. Slowly, she wriggled forward on her stomach until she was between us, then lifted her head to place it on my foot. I reached down to pat her head, rubbing her silk ears and she sighed. Her tail thumped and twitched at intervals.

'Welcome home.' Gabriel's voice was a laughing rumble. 'Another conquest. I can see I'm going to share everything, even my loyal mutt.'

'Told you I'd have her eating out of my hand, didn't I?'

'So you did, witch. Come on, let's go to bed. Hope you don't mind sharing with your new friend. She snores – like you.' Gabriel pulled me out of the chair and into the house, and Jarrah tip-tapped in after us.

The following week Gabriel emptied out a writing desk with brass handles and deep drawers. The bookshelf was already full and I had boxes I hadn't unpacked. I pulled open the smooth drawers and placed the conquistadors inside, along with the Magician's journals and my unsent letters to Gloria. That was when I found it – the tin box Rani had given me, still tied with lace and wrapped in brown paper. I shook it and heard the tiny whisper of its contents – paper, from the sound of it. Well, I had a right to it now. I hadn't seen either aunt or mother for ten years, and even the tax department couldn't hold you to receipts older than seven years. I undid the lace and the paper remained stiffly in place, box-shaped – brown, unyielding paper with a cross marked on its surface. *Promise me you'll never open it. Never look inside. It's important. It's all I have. Promise not to tell anyone. It's our secret.* I heard the voice as clearly as if Rani were beside me, whispering. It was a violation. I shoved the box back in beside the journals. Rani's secret wasn't ready for me.

And there was something else inside the last drawer of my new writing desk, something that wasn't mine – a manila folder with the initial 'C' written in Gabriel's writing. A green manila folder, ordinary and unthreatening, inscribed with the letter 'C'. Handmade origami cards with Japanese writing slid out of the folder and into my hands. Pink cards with multicoloured cranes, red heart-shaped ones with cherry blossoms, marbled silver and gold ones, and a plain white one with a folded flower in the centre. This last one had a message in English, the writing rounded carefully and signed off with six tiny hearts – 'my dearest gabriel how much i miss you i am sending you my heart to keep till we meet again your beloved chiyoko'.

'Who's Chiyoko?' The blunt question leapt into the space between us that evening when Gabriel sat beside me on the verandah, putting down steaming mugs of tea on the table. Jarrah lifted her head and looked at me, wriggling her hind legs to position herself into stillness.

'I beg your pardon.' Gabriel's voice was flat and Jarrah whimpered, dropping her head on her paws.

'Oh my dearest Gabriel, oh how much I miss you, oh please look after my heart till we meet again – *that* Chiyoko. Who is she and when are you planning to return her heart?'

118

'Please don't hold back, Hannah. Just say it. What's really bothering you?' Gabriel bent down to the dog and placed a hand on her head, patting her with a circular motion around her ears.

'I just want to know. Who is she and why haven't you mentioned her?'

'She's none of your business. I'm here with you, aren't I? Why isn't that enough?'

I swallowed a few times, tasting the bitterness at the base of my throat, willing myself into calmness, silence. We sat without speaking till the tea turned lukewarm and Gabriel tipped his mug into the hedge, stood up and said, 'I'm going to read for a while. Don't wait up. Yo, Jarrah. Let's go.'

Jarrah didn't come looking for a spot between us that night. Gabriel slept on his side, facing away from me, saying nothing when I placed my arm over his waist and tried to fit my body around the spaces he left.

Silence wedged itself between us and stalked our days. It followed us to work and stayed with us when we made love. It accompanied us on walks with Jarrah and drank tea with us on the verandah. It stopped his eyes from crinkling at the corners before he smiled. It prevented me from placing the flat of my palm against his forearms. It made him courteous, correct and contained. It made me ill. Silence drowned the rumble of laughter in his throat.

When Clive rang on a Sunday morning to berate me for abandoning him for a better looking bloke, I chattered too much, too insincerely.

'So, are you going to visit us anytime soon?' he asked after the first few minutes of banter.

'I'm so glad you rang, Clive.' My throat closed around the words.

'What's up, kid? Have you had a fight already?'

'Gabriel doesn't fight. He shuts down.'

'All right. Come over. Leanne's home and she'll give you some free advice about men and their deficiencies. Won't you, darling?' Clive's voice was loud while Leanne thumped and clattered in the kitchen, possibly holding up a finger, throwing a tea towel at him.

'Okay,' I said. 'See you soon.'

∞

The front door was open, and I walked straight in to the sound of the phone ringing. The blinds on the windows were raised and the tiles sparkled, still damp. Leanne rarely cleaned, but when she did she was thorough. The smell of bleach and pine disinfectant pricked my nostrils and I called out, 'Phone, Clive, Leanne, it's me.'

'Hannah, grab it, will you? I'm elbow deep in soap suds and Clive's in the loo,' Leanne's voice emerged from the back of the house. I lifted the receiver from its wall cradle and heard the ping-ping of a long-distance call, followed by a beep.

'Call from Tehran,' an Australian voice said cheerfully. 'Tay-ran. Will you accept a reverse-charge call from this number? Yes? Go ahead, ma'am, you can speak now.' The man didn't wait for a response and I heard a click; then nothing for a few seconds and a woman's voice in my ear.

'Hello?' she said. 'So sorry about the reverse charge. Really sorry, but I can explain. It's taken me this long to find you guys. Who's speaking please?' That voice. I hadn't heard it in ten years, never expected to hear it again.

My heart thrummed in my ears like it was dying. 'Who's this?' I asked carefully, flattening my palm against the wall as my head began to pound. Of course it wasn't my sister. The bleach fumes had gone to my head.

'Hannah? Hannah? It's me – Gloria. How are you? Where's Clive? Oh, if you only knew how long it's taken me to track you down – do you know how many Ropers there are in Perth? I even got the Historian one time; luckily it was a machine, so I hung up. Hannah, sweetie, say something.'

Gloria. I opened my mouth and closed it. She went on talking. 'Hannah, I know it's a shock, but please say something.'

'I've just walked in. Clive and Leanne are here too – somewhere. Clive, Leanne, please come to the phone – it's…'

There was a light step behind me and Clive slipped his arm around my waist. I handed him the phone and leaned against him, listening to his heart and his voice. He talked softly and listened, watching me. I tried to stay upright but in the void I saw blood and knew that this time I was awake for the nightmare. Clive put his hand over the mouthpiece and shouted for Leanne. I couldn't move and I couldn't stay still. I fell into that dark pit of blood and screaming children and horned beasts. Sweat drenched me so completely I slipped out of Clive's embrace and sank to the floor with its smell of pine and bleach. Leanne rushed out with a tea towel and scooped me up before my head hit the tiles.

Twenty-eight

'Hannah, listen to me. Think about this. It's not safe. And it's not going to help.' Gabriel sat on our bed and leaned forward, his hair spiky, eyes grim, forehead rumpled.

I looked up from the neat piles of clothes beside an open suitcase. 'I have to go. How can you not see that? I didn't even know she was alive, and now that I know she's in trouble how can you not let me go to her? It's what she would do, in a heartbeat. I owe it to her. You don't know what I owe her.'

'We can get her out of there safely. You don't need to go. She's been living there for years and she can easily arrange to get herself out of there. You don't know if she wants to leave.' Gabriel held his head in his hands briefly before grabbing my arms and stopping me from folding the same shirt over again.

'She cried, Gabriel. Gloria never cries. Okay, she cried once – over me – and all I've done is let her down. I have to go to her. She's in trouble. I have to be there for her. I ruined her life and I'm getting a second chance to make it right.'

'Hannah, you were a child. You didn't ruin her life. She made her own choices. This is an overreaction, don't you think? At least talk to your brothers. I don't see either of them leaping about, sick with worry. Talk to them. Find out what they know. And if you bloody well won't listen, let me go with you.'

'You can't. I have to do this on my own. Please, Gabriel.'

I knelt beside the bed and he lifted me up onto his lap. I put my arms around his neck and we rocked back and forth. I hadn't seen him so disturbed since that Sunday morning in Clive's house when I lay on the couch, tremors still twisting my body. He had taken my hands in his and looked at me as if he were afraid. Then he had kissed me and wiped my face with a crumpled hanky unearthed from his pocket, and my head was so light I didn't make the usual protest. He had smiled briefly and scrunched the hanky back into his jeans.

'Please, Gabriel,' I repeated. 'Let me go. I need to do this. I know she needs me.'

He stopped rocking and became quiet. After a few minutes I slipped off his lap and went back to packing my bag. He watched me. I zipped the bag shut, placed a large silk headscarf in my handbag and looked up.

'Will you take me to the airport or shall I call a cab?'

'I'll drive you.' Gabriel's voice was wretched. He didn't think I would return.

I wanted him back in my arms. I wanted to tell him everything would be okay when I returned with Gloria. We'd get on with our lives and walk with Jarrah under the peppermint and river red gums. Gloria would live with us and find her own Gabriel. Sohrab's revolution would be forgotten. I would not be my mother's daughter. I would come back.

Part III

Revolution

Roya, who forbids me to write, has gone away. I lie alone on the bed we share, without the comfort of her soft body rolling towards me in the middle of the night, her careless arm dropping comfortably over my stomach, her little snores as she settles into her inviolate princess sleep. I think of the bed I shared with Gloria when we were children, until the bedwetting started and Gloria refused to sleep with me. The house is still awake and I know that I am safe. Like the Indian houses, these Persian houses have doors that no one shuts or locks. Like the Indian houses, these have phantoms, ghosts who haunt girl children in the silence of the night.

Twenty-nine

Mehrabad International Airport was festooned with posters of bearded men and curly writing. I adjusted the scarf around my hair and looked for that face. Would I recognise her instantly? Bearded men and shrouded women walked deliberately across the floor as if in a pantomime. Groups of people waited in semicircles with their hands folded in front of them. A man in a safari suit and dark glasses raised his hand in a half-wave. Beside him stood a woman wearing a dark chador. She smiled and held my gaze. I clamped down a surge of nausea as I walked towards them.

'I'm Hamid, *khosh amadid*, welcome,' the man said, his head inclined sideways. 'I am pleased to meet Gulara's sister.' He did not offer to shake hands.

Gulara? The woman folded me into an embrace so hard I forgot to breathe, registering only the stiffness of her clothes and the beat of my heart in my eardrums. She was shorter than me now – rounder, soft-faced and wet-eyed. That was all I could see as we walked out into the grey city. Her hand emerged from her chador and I caught it before she could change her mind. The last time that hand had held mine was when we were children, when the Magician had loved us.

Hamid pointed at a dusty black car and I got into the back while he heaved my case into the boot. I wound down the window and Gloria sat in front with him. They spoke to each other in Farsi. A large brown garment lay on the seat beside me – a chador; was

I supposed to wear it? And this foreign-sounding woman – my sister, my love – was behaving as if this were normal. As if this were something we did regularly – catch up with each other in the Islamic Republic of Iran.

Grim ayatollahs stared at us from walls, flags and posters on terraced houses. All up high. It took a while to realise they were pictures of the same man, the Imam Khomeini himself. He dominated the city, the sides of its buildings, its buses, its shops. That lovely, curly script I had never learned to read accompanied his portraits as we drove through the city. Sohrab used to say Tehran was like Bombay, but I couldn't see any resemblance. Sure, it was dusty and grimy, but in Bombay you wouldn't see gaunt bearded men with guns and quick-stepping shrouded women. Occasionally I saw a sign in English, proclaiming death to the Americans and announcing the long life of the martyrs.

Hamid stopped at a traffic light and switched off the engine. More stubble-faced men carrying guns, women holding boy children firmly by the arm and old men with hunched shoulders walked past. Gloria twisted around. 'Don't worry about that chador, Hannah. It's there – just in case. We shouldn't need it because we won't be stopping along the way – going straight home. I cannot believe you're here.'

'Where are the mountains, the famous Alborz Mountains that Sohrab used to talk about?' I heard my chattering, high voice and bit my lip. My Gloria used to walk with a book on her head and paint her toenails. This Gloria spoke English with a Persian accent.

Before she could reply, Hamid cut in. 'Pollution,' he said with an unpleasant snigger. 'Pollution, rich people and the mullahs – they made the mountains disappear. And the martyrs are all going to the rose garden in the sky.'

'The mountains are to the north of Tehran,' Gloria said calmly. 'We're not going there. We're going to the old part of the city. Maybe we can go to the mountains later.'

Hamid laughed and started the car again. I did not like this man and hoped he would disappear after he had taken us to wherever we were going. We drove through dusty streets where apartment blocks and silver birch grew in communal clumps and empty hammocks stretched across deserted balconies. Bicycles leaned against brick walls covered with ivy, and groups of men appeared out of nowhere, smoking, huddling, turning away. There was safety in numbers, it seemed.

Two hours later we pulled up outside an old house in a dilapidated street where most of the houses looked abandoned. Gloria took a key from the folds of her robe and unlocked the front door. 'There are lots of people in the house – just like India. You'll get used to it. They've all studied in India so they speak English – the young people, I mean. The older ones only speak Farsi,' she said, placing her arm around my waist. 'You'll share a room with Roya. And here she is.' Gloria removed her chador and hung it on a hook behind the door we had just walked through. She wore a plain T-shirt and jeans underneath, her body smaller than I remembered. She turned to embrace a dark-haired girl with thick eyelashes and a shy smile.

'You are welcome, Hannah *jun*,' the girl said, kissing me on both cheeks. 'Gloria has told me all about you. I will also be your sister now.'

'You can call me Maryam,' I said, kissing her back.

'No, no,' the girl laughed. 'We already have two Maryams in the family, so it will be very confusing. They also live with us sometimes. We will call you by your English name. Come.'

Gloria led us through the flaking house with its tiled floors and caramel smell. The walls drizzled plaster on us as we walked, and it stuck to my arms and hair. Roya's room had pink walls and net curtains tied back with bows. A double bed with heart-shaped cushions sat in the middle of the room, and floor cushions lay against the wall. Hamid had already placed my bags by the door.

'We'll talk later,' Gloria whispered, patting my arm. I linked my own through hers and she stopped, an eyebrow raised.

'Gulara?' I asked, and she smiled tightly.

'Some of the men in the family call me that. It's an old Azerbaijani name that sounds like mine. Who would have thought, eh? The Magician must have known, though. I really must go, Hannah. I'll talk to you later.'

'Yes, come, come. I am so happy to see you.' Roya tugged at my hand while smoothing her T-shirt down over her hips, and I became conscious of the elaborate costume I had worn for the journey – long, loose pants and a knee-length shirt buttoned up to my throat and cuffed at my wrists. I pulled off the headscarf as Gloria walked out of the room with her head lowered.

Roya linked arms with me and urged me forward. 'Please be comfortable. Will you have shower? Then we eat. You have come long way and you are tired.'

'Our country is dying,' Hamid said conversationally when Roya and I walked into the front room with the boarded-up window. Four bearded boys looked up at us and away, shyly. Hamid waved his arm towards them. 'We need many good people, many, many young people to make our great country beautiful again. The mullahs are as corrupt as the Shah. We need a new revolution.'

'Ignore him,' Gloria said softly as she stepped forward and embraced me. Roya blushed and looked sideways at Hamid. An old man sat in a wheelchair by the door and stared into the distance, and a woman who looked as if she'd been crying came forward and kissed me on both cheeks.

'Maman *jun*,' Gloria turned to the sad woman and spoke rapidly in Farsi. The woman nodded and stroked my arm, murmuring things that reminded me of the Magician. I understood some of the words – *dokhtar*, the word for 'girl' or 'daughter' – and I absorbed both the magnitude of my self-inflicted journey and the kindness of the woman's words. Sohrab's mother. The one he talked about with the Magician. The one who had lost a son and a daughter to the revolution. The one whose husband sat mutely in a wheelchair. Grief flaked off her like dust. She folded me into her embrace and kissed me again, gesturing with her hand to her mouth that I should eat something.

'Maman *jun*'s heart is broken and Baba's legs don't work,' Hamid reported from his armchair. 'This is what their revolution has given us. Their revolution makes widows of our mothers and sisters and destroys our history and culture. We cannot let that happen. We must fight back.' He stood up and left the room, followed by Roya and the four boys.

'I know,' Gloria held up her right hand and lifted her shoulders in a half-shrug. 'I know he can be tiresome, but he's our cousin and we have to be patient. I mean, he's Sohrab's cousin – Roya has a thing for him.' For an instant there was something of the old mischief in her quick smile, and I squeezed her hand. She sighed and wrapped her arms around me. I smelled honey – Gloria's special scent.

'He sounds like trouble,' I said. 'And who are all those boys?'

'Hamid's okay. He means well, and the boys kind of hero-worship him. Most are from the neighbourhood, some are cousins from Abadan – who knows?'

'And Sohrab?' I asked. 'Is he okay? Is he part of this new revolution?'

'Not really,' she said. 'I'll go and get him.'

'Gloria,' I stopped her. 'Are you married? To Sohrab?'

'Of course I am. This is a Muslim country in the middle of a revolution. You think they'd let me live in sin? We married in Bombay, the same day you left for Australia. I found that out afterwards – we were going to come for you after we were married but Mrs D'Silva told us you'd gone. I missed you and Ammi.'

'So what's going on?' We were both whispering. Baba sat slumped in his chair and Maman *jun* sat beside him, her head bent over a tapestry she took out from a bag slung over the back of Baba's wheelchair. Neither paid any attention to us.

Gloria spread her hands out and looked at the floor. 'Hannah, I don't know where to start. How do I describe ten years on my own with all these people? I thought this was what I wanted. I was so sure that Sohrab and I were…anyway, after Ammi left, I never intended to leave you. Never thought I'd come here and just – you know – stay. We were going to live in Mumbai for a while, going to wait till the fuss died down. We had plans.'

'I thought you hated me – after what I'd done…'

'What? I never hated you. How can I hate you? I was angry. I should have told you, should have realised you were old enough to understand. Like I said, after we married, we were on our way back to Devnagri when we found out about Australia. That horrible Meher person told us. But that was all – we had no address, no phone number, no way of knowing where you'd gone. Australia. That's all we knew. We went back to Bombay and I rang Marina. You remember Marina? Mrs D'Silva's daughter – I'd been living with her after all that stuff happened and the Historian was going to kill Sohrab. Marina said she thought you'd all gone to Perth.' Gloria passed her hand over her eyes in a vaguely familiar gesture and I swallowed an unexpected lump in my throat. My sister was blurring into my mother.

'We must have just missed each other,' I said slowly.

'Yes. I was too young, but thought I was old enough, you know? We didn't have time to do anything because Maman and Baba said we needed to come back – here, to Tehran, because of what happened to Roohi, and life got complicated. Remember how Sohrab used to say if anyone laid a finger on Roohi? It was only by chance that I found Clive – there's a lot…oh God…' she spun around and stepped away from me, eyes fixed on the door.

I turned. An old man with a white stick shuffled in. He wore thick dark glasses and had curly hair – grey, tightly curled hair. He moved towards us with his head tilted to one side, sweeping his stick across the tiled floor like a tap dancer. Gloria flung her arms out and rushed at him.

Once, in the garden at Devnagri the Magician sat with her back to the sun and Matthew Arnold's poems on her lap – and I leaned into her embrace when she read, *'And Sohrab came there, and went in, and stood upon the thick-piled carpets…'*

Thirty

The Historian had known I was stealing money for Sohrab. In a single week I collected 500 rupees, which would have been sufficient to get me to Bombay had I really wanted to go. But I had no idea about buses and trains and locating absconding mothers. Gloria was gone, as was Sohrab and, if I wasn't careful, I'd be the only one left. My brothers watched the Historian as if they expected him to disappear too. I was making it too easy for him to bundle us into a plane and take us to Australia. Divide and conquer. He was, after all, British.

'This isn't your fault, Hannah,' Clive said without conviction on the day the Historian told us we were going to Australia. 'If anything, it's Warren's fault for being a stupid drunk. If he'd kept his mouth shut about Sohrab, Gloria would still be here. And maybe we could have persuaded the old man to let them marry.'

'That's right, Mr Perfect. It must be so comforting to know you're always right.' Warren tossed a cigarette butt into the pond where the turtles used to live. The gardener had removed them just before the Magician disappeared, saying they were too big to live in the little pond and would be released into the lake. He didn't say they would die if they swallowed any more cigarette stubs.

'Well, didn't you convince Gloria that Sohrab was no good?' Clive's voice was stern.

'What did you do, Warren?' I caught my brother's arm and forced him to look at me.

'How old are you now, Hannah? Fourteen? Fifteen?'

'Fifteen,' I said. 'Don't change the subject. Tell me what you did. If you made Gloria run away, you have to make her come back. So we can go to Australia together.'

'I didn't think she really liked him.' Warren lit another cigarette and dragged on it before looking away from me. 'So I told her the truth. It was the truth. I told her that Sohrab…umm…paid for…you know, girls…and he might have diseases. Besides, he's a foreigner and what do we really know about him except what he's told us? If he was doing girls here, he was probably doing them as a teenager in Iran.'

'And how do you know that, Warren?' I let go of his arm. 'Did you two go whoring together?'

'Hannah!' Warren and Clive said at the same time.

'Sorry.' I looked at them until they lowered their eyes and coughed.

'Don't be,' Clive said. 'You're right – but there's no point in blaming each other now. I doubt we can do anything to change the Historian's mind, and if Gloria and Sohrab are meant to be together they'll find a way.'

'How?'

'Sohrab's gone to Bombay. He thinks he has a chance if he speaks to Gloria face to face rather than trying to call her from here. Look, I'm sorry, I was wrong about Sohrab. I made him come with me one time, that's all.' It was Warren this time, smoothing back my hair and throwing away his cigarette. 'With any luck, this will be a lover's tiff and they'll work it out. You can't say anything to the Historian, Hannah, or he'll find a way to stop them. And do something about your hair – it looks like birds are nesting in it.'

'Let's go and bring her back, please? I'll do anything. I've got some of the Magician's jewellery. We can sell that to buy tickets – we can't leave Gloria alone. Anyway, what if she doesn't want to be with Sohrab? We can't leave her without a choice. Mrs D'Silva will help us. Please?' I tugged at Clive's arm.

'Gloria's sensible,' Clive said. 'You know that. She'll be all right. Mrs D'Silva's people are looking after her.'

'So why can't she come with us? We're her family.'

My brothers looked at the ground and Clive hugged me. Warren lit another cigarette and blew the smoke away from my face.

'It's because of me, isn't it?' I asked. 'She won't come because she hates me, because of what I did.'

'That's not it. She doesn't want to come. She wants to stay and make a go of it with Sohrab. She knows if she comes to Australia she'll never see him again. She loves him, Hannah, always has – you need to understand and leave her be.' Clive emphasised his words with his hands, as if waving them towards me would make his message clearer.

My sister, whom I adored almost as much as the missing Magician, had chosen some boy, some homeless, thieving foreign boy, over me. I understood *that*.

Thirty-one

On the balcony of the flat in Mumbai that Gloria shared with two other girls, Sohrab held her hand and cried. 'I didn't betray you,' he said. 'It was once – only once, I swear to you. And I went with your brother. He took me there. I didn't want to go but he made me. You know what Warren is like when he decides to do something.'

'You knew everything, Sohrab. I told you everything. And you still betrayed me.' Gloria ignored his pleas. 'Go away. You're as bad as the Historian. And I'm not a saint like my mother.'

Sohrab came to the flat every day. If Gloria didn't answer the door, her housemates let him in and gave him tea and samosas. They told Gloria she was being too harsh on him. They said he looked like he wasn't getting enough to eat. 'He's living in a *chawl* with some druggie,' they said, clattering teacups in the kitchen. 'Look at the poor boy. It's so romantic – him coming here every day like Majnoo – and you care about him too, don't you? You want him to end up in the gutter with his friend?'

'Not my problem. If you're so keen, you look after him. You can feed him and marry him for all I care,' Gloria said crossly, but she watched Sohrab drink tea in a big gulp and push his glasses up on his nose. She saw the too-large shirt he'd been wearing for three days in fetid pre-monsoon Mumbai. 'Where are you staying, Sohrab?' she asked as he was leaving, head down, face flushed, shirt limp with sweat.

Sohrab took off his glasses and wiped his eyes. 'With my friend, Mehran. He is good to me,' he said slowly. 'He does not have money, but he has many troubles, like me. Thank you for tea. I am very grateful.'

'Come and have dinner with us tomorrow, Sohrab. And bring your friend. We'll try and work something out.'

Sohrab smiled, bowed and skipped out, and Gloria's roommates laughed and said Laila had been reconciled with Majnoo.

He didn't come the following day. Or the day after. Or the one after that. Gloria told her flatmates never to mention his name again. On the fifth morning Mehran turned up, pressing the bell repeatedly and begging her to come with him.

'You must come. You must come. Sohrab is on the floor and cannot get up.' Mehran had wild black hair and intense brown eyes ringed with pink. He shifted from foot to foot and smoked a foul-smelling *bidi*.

'What happened? Did he fall over?'

'I don't know. I am not doctor. He send me to you. You must come.'

The *chawl* was seedy, filled with sour drunk men who beat their women noisily in the alleyways. Naked children played near open drains and fought for food with the street dogs. It was the first time Gloria had ever set foot in a neighbourhood like that. She held her dupatta over her nose and stepped over human and animal dung on her way to the single room where Sohrab lay, shaking and odorous, on a thin, stained mattress. She looked around and wondered where he washed – if he washed. She said she would help him if he returned to the flat with her but he refused. So she went back to the *chawl* with a doctor.

'Malnourished,' said the doctor, with a quick look around the room. 'What are you two doing in a place like this? This poor man – Iranian, isn't he? – needs to be with his own people. All I can do is give him a vitamin shot and an antibiotic, but he needs lots of fresh fruit and clean water, or he's just going to get worse. Especially if he's eating food he's not used to.'

Gloria blamed herself for being so full of anger she hadn't seen the state Sohrab was in. She went to the *chawl* every day with fresh fruit and water and a thermos of tea and sat with him while he ate and drank. She gave Mehran some money to buy him clean clothes and a mattress and asked the doctor to check on him again. After a week Sohrab sat up, polished his glasses and apologised for being a nuisance.

'Please come back to the flat with me, Sohrab,' Gloria said again. 'You can't be healthy if you live here. This place, it's terrible – not fit for human beings.'

'So what am I then, animal?' Mehran spat on the ground and looked at them with red eyes. He had been simmering for days, watching Gloria and her friends fuss over Sohrab. 'I look after him like a brother and you come with your fruit and clothes and tell me I'm no good?'

'Mehran, you know Sohrab needs help and you can't look after him. I'm doing you both a favour. You don't have to live here – you can find somewhere else. I need to look after Sohrab.'

'No, no. I will look after *you*. I am well now, see?' Sohrab swayed a little as he stood up and held his hand out to Gloria. They stepped over dog shit and drunken men and crying children, and walked out of the stinking alley, Mehran still grumbling and shouting that Sohrab was not welcome in his house any more.

Gloria's voice was steady. She had recounted this before: to my brothers, to Sohrab's parents, to anyone who asked.

'And then?' I asked.

'And then he and I got married and came to Iran. Ten years ago.'

'And now?' It seemed I was only capable of two-word sentences, but Gloria nodded and stroked my arm.

'Now? Well, he can't see very much. His eyesight deteriorated when we came here and there was no money for specialists or anything – and after Roohi died, it was like he didn't want to see any more. Oh, it was horrible to see Maman stand over Roohi's body and cover it with her chador. And Sohrab next to her and Baba refusing to speak – how could I say I missed my family when their daughter had been killed? And Reza too, the brother Sohrab was closest to – he's dead. All this tragedy, such a waste, and here I am in the middle of it.'

'It's okay – I'm here too. You're not alone.'

Gloria continued to stroke my arm, the way the Magician used to. 'I'm tired,' she said. 'I don't know what I'm doing any more. I'm tired of this country and this language. I want to walk without a shroud on my head.'

'Let's get out of here. Come back with me. That's what you want, don't you?'

Gloria looked towards the door before nodding. 'You know how the aunties used to talk about sending Sohrab back to his own people? And how upset we all were? They were right. Everyone needs their own people. And these are not my people. I'm sick of their revolution – their…their courage, their bloody poetry; when things are bad they recite Rumi and Hafez. I wait for midnight knocks on the door. I call Khomeini's boys my brothers. I don't want this any more. I want to find Ammi.' She stooped into my arms and I held her. She was warm, honey-soft, tired. But she was finally my Gloria.

'Let's do it, then. I want to find Ammi, too. One small step at a time. Let's get you out of Iran first.'

If I felt a twinge of guilt about Sohrab, I crushed it underfoot, like the cigarettes he used to smoke.

Thirty-two

The Magician was in her kitchen, humming a familiar song under her breath, stirring something. She grated ginger into a pot of simmering liquid and added turmeric root and threw in a handful of leaves that made the water green.

I peered in, breathing in the fumes and blinking. 'What is that? Are we planning to kill something with it?'

'Very funny, my Maryam. Here – taste some.' I squealed as the Magician dipped a spoon into the pot and held it towards me. She laughed and put a lid on the pot, then switched off the stove. 'You won't recognise it when you see it next – it will be as tasty as halva and you will beg me for more. Now go and get Sohrab for me, please.'

'Why do you always want Sohrab? Why can't you and me and Gloria be like we were? You never ask for Clive and Warren and they are your real sons, aren't they?'

The Magician must have been in a good mood because she kissed my cheek and repeated her request.

I found Sohrab in his usual spot beside the pond, smoking and staring into the distance, the transistor chattering on the parapet. The BBC reported relentlessly on the state of the revolution, which was now in its second month. The Americans were furious.

Israel was on high alert. The Arabs were encouraging Saddam across the border. The BBC did not have any news about all the babas and maman *juns* in Iran who waited for their sons and daughters. Sohrab's cheeks were stubbly with a week's growth and his forehead creased with squinting at the Indian sun. He was a stranger now, his giggling, brotherly attitude a thing of the past. He spent too much time with Warren and smelled odd, some days.

'Ammi wants you,' I said, pity chasing away the jealousy of a moment ago.

'*Where is sermon and hymn and the violin's music whence? Upon seeing our friend, our foes put up their defence,*' he said, throwing down the cigarette and stamping on it twice.

'What?'

'Hafez. That is famous poem by Hafez, you know? He was Sufi from Shiraz and he wrote many beautiful poems. When I am troubled I read his poetry. I have English translation if you want, Maryam.'

'Sohrab, the Magician is looking for you,' I said as he continued to stare into the distance.

'I will come now,' he took out his lighter and flicked it on and off and put it back inside his pocket. 'You must read Hafez.'

Gloria and the Magician were spreading a translucent green liquid into flat trays and dropping little slivers of almonds over the rapidly setting mixture when I went back with Sohrab.

'I don't care how pretty it looks,' I said, scrunching my nose. 'I'm not eating that.'

'Nobody's asking you to.' Gloria threw a twig of almond in my direction and I ducked. 'This is for Sohrab. It's full of good things to help him heal.'

'And forget,' the Magician said, so softly that only I heard.

Thirty-three

Roya's room was a young girl's room – pink walls and beaded curtains around a freestanding mirror. I remembered my dream of sharing a house with Gloria. A house with white-framed windows and silk curtains tied back with bows. A tiny house, too small for cousins and aunties and hangers-on. A house for the two of us. Antisocial, Gloria had called me then. And now here I was, trying to smuggle her out of a country neither of us had known about when we waited for that school bus on the road that wasn't quite a road, the Magician's cautions ringing in our ears.

What would the Magician have said to me that night as I contemplated betrayal and deception? Betrayal of hospitality was a greater sin in the Magician's book than any other. And Roya, whose large, soft bed I shared, was nothing if not hospitable. After making sure I was comfortable, covering me gently when the blanket slipped off, she whispered her feelings about Hamid to me at night. 'He's good boy,' she said. 'We will make Iran better because we have people like him to guide us. But I think he is wrong to get mixed up with those Abadani boys. They are too much like Arabs even though they are Persian – and we cannot trust them. We must be careful. All the foreigners, they make more trouble. Not like you and my lovely Gloria. Our people are the same, you know? You are both almost Persian, and now we are family.'

'Thank you, Roya, but aren't we all in enough trouble? I mean, I don't agree with Hamid and his new revolution,' I said, rolling on my side to face her. She was really lovely, even in the gloom, with her dimples and thick hair and vanilla-scented skin. Lovely, but deluded: Hamid was a lunatic and she thought he was going to save them. Some hero he was – with his borrowed rhetoric and sly alcoholism. I recognised the signs: the excessive politeness, the overpowering aftershave, the constant gum-chewing. Warren used to smell like that and smile with pink-tinged eyes. But Warren didn't fancy himself a revolutionary and quote from *Mein Kampf.*

'Yes, I know. But the heart knows what it wants, yes?' Roya touched my cheek with the back of her hand. 'I know you are thinking about poor Sohrab *jun*. Your sister is so patient. We are blessed. She is the only reason he is alive. He lives for her. When Khoda sent us Gloria, Maman *jun* said it was like her own daughter had come back. And after Roohi became martyr, your sister keeps us all together. It's a beautiful story, Sohrab and Gloria – like *Leili and Majnun*. Our Persian poet Rumi says when we belong to the soul of the beloved, we are neither body nor soul. Your sister and Sohrab are like that. They belong to each other – one soul – beautiful, yes?'

I yawned, patted her hand and said I was going to sleep. It wouldn't do for me to talk about Sohrab and Gloria in the same way as the fabled lovers to whom Roya had dreamily referred.

A month after Gloria had drooped into my arms with a sigh, I told her we needed to ring Clive. We had not spoken again of leaving – somehow we were always interrupted, sometimes by Sohrab and sometimes by the sad-faced women who came to have tea with Maman *jun*. Gloria asked me to be patient and I asked her if she had changed her mind.

'No,' she said, looking away from me.

I phoned Clive two weeks later, when the house had emptied of young revolutionaries and only Baba sat in his wheelchair in the front room. Gloria listened out for Sohrab tapping along in the corridor and I made the reverse-charge call.

'I agree,' said Clive. 'Go to Mumbai first and I'll get a visa for Gloria. She can come here with you and we can apply to have her here permanently – family reunion and all that. There's no way we could bring Sohrab over, especially if he's as sick as you say he is.'

I glanced towards Gloria before saying, 'Of course.'

'Hannah, you're sure Gloria wants this? There's no going back for her. Make sure she understands that. And don't get sidetracked. Please. Just get out of Iran and come here. Get back to Perth. We – Gabriel and us – we miss you, so hurry up.'

My stomach knotted and I thought about leaving Sohrab, unknowing, on his own. 'Tell him…tell Gabriel I'll be home soon,' I said to my brother.

They came in the middle of the night. They kicked at the door until Maman *jun* started wailing and Roya and I tumbled from our room with our arms around each other, in time to see the door crash inwards. They wore navy shirts tucked into their pants and carried rifles they pointed at us as they shouted. One soldier flooded the room with light and gestured to someone behind him.

Roya threw a chador over my head and another over herself and said, 'Don't look at them. Don't say anything. They are looking for the boys. You are safe. Even these *shaitoon* will not touch a visitor.' She lowered her head. I did the same. A sound beside me and Gloria appeared, shrouded and downcast – then Maman *jun*, quiet now – and the two little girls who were visiting from Abadan. Everyone seemed calm, and the little girls came over to stand in front of me, protectively. This was a country where the visitor was second only to God. The phrase in Farsi they used translated loosely as: 'We are honoured to place your feet on our head.' I hugged the girls and felt their small bodies press into mine.

The men went through the house, banging on walls and kicking furniture. Glass shattered in the kitchen and the children burrowed into us. Baba called out and Maman *jun* sat down on the floor, holding her head in her hands. I made a fist of my right hand and breathed in. That pig, Hamid – this was his fault. If it weren't for his stupid meetings over chai and slabs of *barbari* with bearded students, this would not be happening. Where was he – the hero of the revolution – while we were being terrorised? I hoped they would find him and slap him around.

'We'll be okay, Hannah,' Gloria said in my ear. 'This is a regular thing. They won't find anything and they'll go away.'

The soldiers talked loudly to each other. One of them wheeled Baba into the room and spun him around, laughing. Roya dug her fingers into my arm as I tensed. Sohrab shuffled in without his stick, palming the wall with his left hand, calling out to Gloria.

'Oh, Gloria, Gloria, Gloria,' the guards chanted and Sohrab froze. Gloria took his arm and led him to a chair beside Baba, whispering in his ear.

The soldier who had pushed Baba stared at Gloria, then at us. He said something in Farsi and she responded.

'So,' said the guard in English. 'A spy who speaks our language – very clever. Clever Israeli spy.'

'No, brother,' Gloria said. 'I am not Israeli. I am Muslim. I have given up my family and my country to live here. I am a daughter in this house. Please ask that brother there' – she pointed to a tall guard leaning against the mantelpiece, watching. 'That brother has seen my papers. We have nothing – we have given everything to the revolution.'

'That is right,' the tall guard said, also in English. 'I have seen the papers. All women here, like this one' – he walked up to Sohrab and slapped his face. Sohrab's glasses fell off and he groped around for them, eyes staring straight ahead. The guard kicked away the glasses and continued, 'Tell me, *khanum*, where is your brother Hamid? Is he hiding under your skirts? Or are you dumb as well as blind?'

Roya flung my arm away and marched up to the guard. She placed herself in front of Sohrab, who raised an arm over his face as if expecting another blow. She spoke to the soldiers directly, making eye contact. Her normal voice, with its happy rhythm, was replaced by a flat drone I couldn't recognise even had I understood the words. The soldiers crowded around her, shooting questions at her, their voices harsh. She nodded several times. They formed a circle around her while urging her forwards, moving her towards the gaping doorway and into the night.

Maman *jun* started wailing again and Sohrab looked around and pushed at air. Baba slumped forward in his chair and wheeled himself away from the room. Maman *jun* followed him, moaning and beating her chest with a small fist.

'Come and help me, Hannah,' Gloria said. 'The door – we have to fix it somehow.'

The little girls helped. We picked up the door and heaved it back into position. Gloria looped a length of wire through the gaps between the frame and door and wedged it in place. We moved chairs and tables and chests of drawers in front of it as a barricade. We swept up glass from the kitchen floor and found some cups that had survived.

I made tea, Indian-style – boiling the milk with tea leaves, cardamom, cloves, ginger and sugar. I took it to the room with the boarded-up windows and placed a cup in Sohrab's hand. I sat on the floor beside him and he touched my head briefly. 'How are your brothers?' he asked, and I talked to him for the first time since coming here. I told him about Clive and Leanne and Warren and Gabriel and the red dog who wriggled into position near our feet when we sat down to eat.

'*Death came, smelled me, and sensed your fragrance instead,*' Sohrab replied.

'Rumi or Hafez?' I asked.

'Yes,' said Sohrab and drooped on the broken chair. I continued to sit cross-legged on the floor, while he recited poetry in short, ragged bursts, his head sinking low into his chest. I tried to see the man Gloria had fallen in love with – he was only thirty-five after all, despite his white hair and stooped back and thin hands that shook when he lifted the teacup to his lips. I steadied that hand and asked him if he had a spare pair of glasses somewhere. He shook his head and turned his face away.

Gloria gathered the girls to her and murmured something in their ears. They nodded and wiped their eyes and held her hand. Maman *jun* clattered into the room and rushed towards Gloria, holding her fiercely, smoothing hair away from her forehead, tucking it back under the chador.

We waited for morning. Two curly-haired girls slept on the floor with their arms around each other. No one told me where Roya had gone or when she would come back. Sohrab and Gloria went to their room and I stared at the door behind the barricade, wondering how we would get out.

Thirty-four

Despite the serenity the Magician had tried to foster, ours was a disordered household. There were too many of us, and we didn't know how everyone fitted into our lives. The Magician's parents had died when she was barely a teenager. She had grown up with some of the aunties and cousins who visited us regularly. Meher was her cousin, extraordinary though the thought was. Their fathers were brothers and the Magician had lived in Meher's house after the death of her own parents. How our beautiful Magician could have the same blood as that woman was a question we asked each other often as children, especially after one of Meher's pinches or slaps. It was bad enough that the Historian was a freak who locked up his only sister. Once, I decided I wanted to give him other siblings for the sake of normalcy. Gloria overheard me telling a classmate about my father's brothers and sisters in England. She slapped my hand and told me to hold my tongue.

'What is wrong with you? Why must you make up stories? Don't we have enough dramas in our lives already? If the Magician finds out, she'll —'

'Don't tell her, Gloria. But don't you think it strange that we don't have any real aunties and uncles?'

'We've got Rani.'

And in that Persian house, after Roya disappeared, I understood the presence of strangers and relatives in families like ours. Silent, guarded women brought fruit and biscuits for Maman *jun* and wept with her. They helped her with her tapestry and filled bowls with pomegranate and cucumbers. They drank chai and murmured *merci* after they hugged and kissed each other on both cheeks. Sometimes they took Maman *jun* away and she returned at the end of the day with slumped shoulders and tears folded inside the wrinkles on her cheek.

Men whose faces looked older than their years wheeled Baba to the windowless room and smoked listlessly. One of them fixed the door and reinforced it with a frame that looked as if it could withstand an earthquake – all without saying a word. The bearded boys disappeared and Hamid's name was never mentioned. Sometimes I heard Roya's name being whispered when Maman *jun* was away, and I wondered where my dear dimpled friend was and how she coped with whatever had happened to her. When I asked Gloria, she shushed me and wiped her eyes and I dared not ask again.

Gloom stuck to the walls and drizzled down on us when we moved through, and I became afraid. So afraid. I clung to the side of Roya's bed at night and prayed I wouldn't have another nightmare. I had screamed and woken up the night after the guards came, and when Gloria had insisted on sleeping with me I pretended not to notice the fresh smell of sex on her. But I judged; oh, how I judged her – how *could* she? After what had happened?

I followed Gloria, scrubbing and cleaning and cooking with her – watching. Once, after the chores were done and we were sipping tea in the kitchen, I asked her about the afternoons we had spent reading Grandfather's diaries.

'Why did Grandfather Billy kill himself? You never told me.'

Gloria flicked a tea towel at me. 'Feeling cheerful today? What a thing to ask, after all these years, Hannah.'

'Well?'

'I have no idea. He wrote in his diaries for thirty years – then he stopped. He didn't say why he was going to kill himself or when. If I had to guess, I'd say he was depressed. I don't think he was a planner. It must have been horrible for the Historian, to have been the one who found him.'

'Gabriel's dad did the same thing. But he was living on his own at the time, so neither Gabriel nor his mum saw him – which is a small blessing, I suppose.'

Gloria hugged me tight. 'I promise you this. I will get you out of here. This time I'll look after you properly.'

'What if you'd come with us to Australia instead?'

'Sohrab would have died. Don't judge me, Hannah. He's my husband.' Gloria kept a hand on my arm, and the look in her eyes told me she knew what I was thinking.

Feeling small, I looked away.

Nine days later, Gloria and I walked out of the house in the morning. We stuffed a few things in small bags under our chadors, including all the Australian and Indian money I had, divided equally, in case we were separated. We left our hairbrushes and toothbrushes, our clothes hanging on hooks and in wardrobes, our inside slippers by the door – if anyone wondered, we were just going to the market.

There was no question any more of attempting to leave by plane. The Islamic Republic did not take kindly to foreign women trying to leave their country without papers. While my passport was intact, Gloria had nothing. Both her Indian passport and her stamp of residency in Iran were torn up in front of her by the tall guard in the last raid, before I came. That was when, scared and broke, she had phoned us. Now, after the midnight raid, we knew we were watched, and our only hope were the strangers who would, for a fee, smuggle us out of Iran. By choosing to do this, my sister and I became what Australians would later call 'queue jumpers'. Not that I had seen any queues with women anywhere in this country of bearded, gun-toting men and chanting revolutionaries.

A car idled by a side road and we got in, filling the space with our too-loud breathing. The driver and the man sitting beside him didn't turn around but drove on, slowly at first, then faster as we cleared the crowded bazaar and moved onto the highway. A rough basket filled with water, cheese, bread and blankets sat near our feet, and the driver's friend passed us two frayed chadors whose hems were stiff with mud.

'Leave your good chadors in the car. Wear these. You must look like you come from farming families.' The man's voice was courteous.

We did as instructed and watched the speeding trees as the driver accelerated and turned on the radio. Above the static the men talked quickly. The names of cities rolled off their tongues – Kermanshah, Yazd, Bandar Abbas, Zahedan. I gripped Gloria's hand and leaned towards her. She drew my head down onto her shoulder. I remembered Sohrab circling cities with a red ballpoint pen when the revolution robbed him of words. We rushed out of his country with our eyes closed and our hearts thumping.

We woke to silence. It was dark and cold, a sliver of moon glinting low over an unknown sky. The men leaned against the bonnet, the red tips of their cigarettes curving rapidly back and forth. They straightened when we got out and stubbed out their cigarettes.

'You must eat,' said the man who had spoken earlier. 'It is a long journey and you may have to walk. But first we eat and then we wait. The next car is late.'

I took out the cheese and the flatbread and found some herbs wrapped in a tea towel as well as yoghurt, plums and dates. The men spread out a blanket beside the car and we sat down and ate. It was too dark to be sure, but it felt like we were in a field – the ground beneath our feet was soft and dusty. I thought I heard night birds but everything else was quiet and still. The men brought out a thermos filled with fragrant Persian tea – too sweet and lukewarm, but we drank it anyway.

The car we were waiting for was really a van, already full when it sputtered towards us. A man got out from the front and waved us in. I got in first and sat beside the driver, who smelled of sheep and smoke and wore a baseball cap. Behind us were huddled figures – all women and children.

'Thank God there aren't any men,' Gloria said softly and I nodded, then realised she probably couldn't see in the dank interior, so I whispered back a faint yes.

The van made slow progress, primarily because it bumped over fields and small hills. Gloria spoke to the driver in Farsi, listening quietly to his grunted replies.

'He thinks we'll be in Pakistan in a couple of hours,' she said in my ear. 'Then we wait for his contact and go to Karachi. We split up after this. The people in the back are one family but they will have to go their separate ways and meet up later.'

A little boy coughed behind us, a thick, phlegmy cough, and his mother shushed him, drawing his head into her lap. Another woman started humming softly and the boy quietened, with the cough surfacing every few minutes until he fell asleep. A low conversation started up behind us and Gloria strained to hear.

'I think they are trying to decide whether the mother should stay with the little boy or go with the teenage daughter,' Gloria told me. 'The other lady is her sister-in-law – the one who was singing, but she doesn't speak any Urdu and neither does the girl, so they're nervous.'

'Can we help them?' My throat was dry and I needed a drink but there wasn't a thermos or bottle of water to be seen anywhere.

'Best not to get involved,' Gloria said flatly.

The morning sky was pink through the dusty windows of the van as it hurtled towards what I hoped was the border. We had driven all night and the driver had smoked incessantly, making the boy cough even more. The women had given up trying to keep him quiet, although the mother chanted prayers softly, reminding me of the Magician. I kissed Gloria and smelled the driver's smoke in her hair.

We turned into a narrow lane with a few huts scattered along its path. Men pushing handcarts filled with vegetables and sleepy children slowed us down to a crawl. We lowered our heads and I wished I had the anonymity of the chadors that lay discarded in the back. We turned a corner into an open field and the car accelerated again, throwing us against each other. The little boy whimpered and the mother said something to the driver, who reached under his seat and passed a bottle of water to her. The children drank first, then the women and I tapped the driver on the arm, miming a drink. He reached under his seat again and brought out another bottle, only a quarter full, and Gloria and I had a sip each and passed it back to him.

'*Merci*,' I said, and he nodded.

'Balochistan,' he said, pointing ahead and we looked. The sky lost its pretty pink streak and turned white. The countryside was familiar and strange – tarmac roads with fields on either side, women bent over neat rows of vegetables and men pushing carts across worn paths. We drove on until we saw a petrol station and the driver stopped and got out.

A young girl wearing a flower-print shalwar and man's shirt came running from inside a squat whitewashed barn, pulled open the doors and urged us out, tugging at our hands when we hesitated. In Urdu she said, 'Come in – come out – quickly – you must – now – come, come.' The driver disappeared.

The women in the back got out silently. The coughing boy doubled over in the dust and had to be carried by his mother. Gloria and I followed them to the barn. I touched the money belt under my kurta and drew my dupatta around me like a shawl. My mouth was woolly and I wanted toothpaste. A small group of children jumped inside the van as soon as we left it and searched it, shouting when they found empty water bottles and cigarette stubs under the front seat. They threw the bottles out and pushed the car to the back of the building.

'Welcome,' a smiling woman dressed entirely in white said to us as we entered the barn. She squatted in front of a small primus stove on which she was cooking chapattis. The girl who had pulled us from the van poured steaming tea into glasses and beckoned us to a plastic-covered table with cane stools arranged around it and we sat down quickly. The girl placed the tea in front of us and we sipped. Hot, thick, sweet tea had never tasted better. Our last cup had been by the road somewhere on the border between Iran and Pakistan, two nights ago.

Thirty-five

'Tell me about Perth,' Gloria said. 'What's the best thing about it?'

'It's clean and quiet and empty – you'll notice how quiet. I used to shout and clap my hands when we first got there, just for the heck of it. The Historian's house is on a big block and I didn't see anyone initially except for Aunty Frankie and the girls.'

Gloria watched me, hand cupping her chin. This was the first time she'd mentioned Perth. I took it as a good sign and chattered on. 'The trees smell of peppermint. The cockatoos – they're like white parrots – remind me of us when we were kids: they're noisy and they sit in trees and chuck down flowers and seeds. And yes, kookaburras do laugh. It's more of a cackling, really – the way the aunties used to cackle. Oh, you'll have to get used to the light – I can't tell you what that's like. It's everywhere. Perth wouldn't be a good place to hide because the light gets into everything and hunts you down. Aunty Frankie told me to invest in a good pair of sunnies if I didn't want to look like an old woman by the end of summer – best advice ever.'

Gloria raised a hand over her eyes. 'I'm an insomniac now,' she said. 'Remember how you used to complain that I could sleep through anything? The light won't bother me. I rest with my eyes open.'

There wasn't much light in this high-walled room in Karachi. We had been driven here at night three days ago. A woman brought us food three times a day and hot bathwater in buckets at ten am. She locked us in when she left. The Iranian family with the coughing boy had disappeared, and our tight-lipped hostess shook her head when I asked what happened to them. 'You will be in Hindustan soon,' she said curtly. 'Find your people and forget what you've seen.'

'Gloria,' I sat on the cot beside her and she shifted to make room for me. 'We will get out of here. They need to get us out of here to make room for the next lot. Don't worry.'

'I know,' she said. 'I'm sorry to have dragged you into this. If Ammi knew...'

'You can't be responsible for me all your life. And you didn't drag me into anything. I came to get *you*, remember?'

A quick rap on the door made us look at each other. Gloria scooped up the dupatta hanging on a nail behind the bed and I covered my head before opening the door. A dark boy with a pencil moustache and a baseball cap was outside. Our hostess stood beside him and pointed at a battered yellow van. 'Time to go,' she said. '*Khuda Hafiz*. May God go with you.' And she held out her hand, open-palmed. I put money into her hand and the boy held open the door to the van. As soon as we were inside he took off in a storm of dust so thick we couldn't see anything until our eyes adjusted. Next stop, India – we hoped.

Thirty-six

Jarrah followed me everywhere, sitting outside the toilet, waiting by the gates as I drove in, jumping on the chair beside me when I watched TV, flopping down on the kitchen floor and getting in my way. Summer lingered, bringing long days of intense sunlight and clarity. The hills were quiet, except when the cockatoos sailed home over the trees at the end of the day and the crickets started their click-clack. Gabriel worked in the shed until seven in the evening, coming in only when I called out to him or when Jarrah scratched at the door. He watched me – but looked away if I caught him out. Sometimes he would lean over to touch my arm or hold my hand, avoiding my eyes. He watched Gloria too – but gently, without anger.

'What is it, Gabriel?' I asked one evening in the kitchen when he straightened from the fridge with a beer, looking around for a stubby holder. I tossed one at him and he wedged his stubby of Emu Bitter inside and leaned back against the benchtop. 'Why won't you look at me properly? Have I grown a pair of horns only you can see? A mole? Scaly skin? You don't look at me and you barely touch me. If you've changed your mind about us...'

'How can you say that? You – who took off on a harebrained mission to rescue your sister, who smuggled her into the country illegally on a fake visa, who expects that everything's going to be just as it was before. I don't get it. How can you be so okay? This isn't a normal situation, Hannah, and you insist on behaving as if it is.' Gabriel swallowed a large mouthful of beer before tipping the rest of it into the sink. I regretted the waste. Beer made a good hair conditioner and, if he wasn't going to drink it, I could have used it. He thumped the stubby down on the bench. The window behind him lit up his hair and turned it gold. He stared ahead, his face in shadow.

'So what bothers you most? That I saved my sister's life or that she's here on a bought visa?'

'I'm not sure I like that tone, Hannah.'

'And I'm not sure why I'm arguing with someone who clearly hasn't got a clue about what life is like for women in dangerous places. I think you're worried about the unwashed hordes taking over your precious country, because who knows how many more can get in here after Gloria?'

'How dare you accuse me of being a redneck. How dare you make this about race. We have rules for a reason. If everyone ran around doing what they needed to do because their relatives are in trouble in a foreign country, we'd have chaos. We'd *be* that foreign country people are so eager to leave. You hypocrite. And your sister is not the problem.' Gabriel's voice was loud in the tiny kitchen.

'Gabriel.' But he was gone. The sink smelled of beer when I turned on the tap.

Winter arrived one morning in a slick of cold rain and tree-bending winds. Everyone talked about how unpredictable Perth was becoming, weather-wise. 'What's happened to those lovely autumn days,' colleagues at work asked, grumbling and stamping their feet on the square outside the State Library, pulling their coats around them.

One Saturday in April, on a rostered day at work, I saw a familiar figure standing outside the coffee kiosk with a large canvas under her arm. I almost ran into the foyer, away from her. Then

I stopped, retraced my steps and stood behind her in the queue. I touched her upper arm and she turned to face me, eyebrow lifted, purple lips curling at the corners.

'Hello, Anya. How are you?'

'Hannah.' The voice flat, eyes flickering quickly over my navy skirt and jacket, her hand thrust inside the pocket of a paint-stained windcheater. 'What are you doing here?'

'I work here.' I waved an arm towards the glass doors and grey carpets behind us. 'And you?'

'I paint here.' She pointed at the square outside the Art Gallery. 'I'm having an exhibition soon. You should come.'

'I'd love to – where?'

'It'll be in the papers. Look me up.' We were at the counter now. She put down the canvas and waved a languid hand at someone I couldn't see, digging into her pockets for money. She paid for her coffee, picked up the canvas and walked away without a backward glance. I placed my order and watched her disappear into the crowds surging towards the shops.

I would look her up. If she really were having an exhibition I would take Gloria with me to see her paintings. I would mention, lightly, the mad artist with whom I'd once shared a house. I wouldn't say anything about the dreams that now featured a skinny girl wearing purple lipstick, the girl who laughed, and died.

I worried about Gloria experiencing Perth's winter for the first time, and carried a coat and a couple of thick cardigans over my arm for her. She felt the cold in her bones, like the Magician.

Gloria divided her time between Clive's place and ours – I still thought of it as ours, despite Gabriel's silence and Jarrah's wet-eyed reproach. I didn't know how to fix things with either of them, so I did what the Magician had taught – cooked and cleaned and read.

In Clive's driveway, I shivered and rehearsed what I needed to say. Gloria's time in Perth was running out – she had two months left before she had to return to India. She had insisted only that she did not want to see the Historian. She did not feel ready, she said. Apart from that, she fitted into our lives quietly, like loss.

'She's not like you at all.' Leanne twisted her cigarette butt into the wilting fuchsia outside their front door and took my arm. 'I mean, you look like sisters, for sure, but she seems...so foreign somehow, you know? So quiet – hard to know what she's thinking, what she's been through.'

I nodded. 'I keep waiting for the real Gloria to stand up and announce something. Do you think she should see a psychologist or someone who specialises in trauma? Maybe Clive could —?'

'I was thinking the same thing.' Leanne pushed open the front door. 'She should see a professional. I'll get Clive to talk to her. He'll be discreet. And how long do you think you can avoid dear Papa? I know she doesn't want to see him, but we can't hold him off forever.'

'I'll talk to him.'

Gloria was here, with me, and she was safe. Not even the Historian could change that.

'I don't need a psychologist, you silly things.' Gloria sat in the recliner by the bay window and looked at us, her face open, a smile starting in her eyes. She stood up and hugged me. 'Hannah, I'm older than you and you're not allowed to worry about me – that's my job. I'm fine. Still adjusting, you know. Sorry I've been —'

I put my arm around her. 'Gloria, we didn't mean to imply —'

'It's okay. I know I've been a bit self-absorbed. I wanted to be sure...but seeing as you're all here – Hannah, you're going to be an aunty. A bit inconvenient, all things considered, but there you go.'

The rain stopped and the sun came out, sending planks of sunlight across the room, striping our faces as we looked at each other.

'Shit,' said Leanne and clamped her hand to her mouth. Gloria spread her hands out and Clive leaned across and took them in his own.

The Historian. He would know what to do about visas and babies. There was no way I was letting Gloria out of my sight now.

Thirty-seven

'Bugger off! I mean it, Hannah. Don't say another word. *You* need a shrink, not your sister. She's okay but you're losing the plot.'

'Gabriel, just listen, please?'

'No. You're insane.' Gabriel looked at me as if I had grown scales. Two lines creased his forehead an angry red and he breathed hard. Jarrah whimpered. Automatically, he reached for her and ran his fingers over her head. When he looked at me again, his eyes were icy. 'It's over, Hannah. I'm sorry. I know you want the best for your sister but your obsession is scary. You really do need help. And the sad thing is you don't even know how crazy you sound. Do us a favour – don't talk to anyone else.' He patted the dog and urged her out the door. A minute later I heard the thrum of his bike and he roared off down the driveway.

Was it so extraordinary, what I had asked him to do? It was only temporary and it was the perfect solution. People who loved each other ought to help each other. 'It's over,' he had said. He didn't mean it – how could he? Into every life a little rain must fall. And a lot of rain was falling over us now, but it would stop. Surely Gabriel, with his Australian disregard for rules, would be happy to thumb his nose at authority? They never had to wait in queues, these Australians – they had never learned the fundamental art of patience. They made decisions. They went out and got what they wanted. They hated rules – until someone from somewhere else tried to break them. Something was definitely bothering Gabriel. And it wasn't me.

I wandered around inside the house for a while, let Jarrah in, made myself a cup of coffee and shared a piece of buttered toast with her. She followed me into the study and jumped up on the chair by the window.

'It's okay,' I said. 'He'll be back. We'll be okay.' Jarrah pointed her ears briefly and let them flop. The look on her face told me I was dreaming.

I pulled open the drawer with the Magician's journals and flipped through them. I should get Gloria to read these. She would know what all that curly writing meant. There was a hollow sound as I shut the drawer, so I pulled it open again and stared at Rani's box. Faded somewhat, missing the brown paper and the lace ribbon. I shook it once, as I had done earlier before being distracted by Chiyoko's letters to Gabriel. Those letters were long gone and I hadn't questioned their absence.

The tin lid was rusty where it met the latch. It wouldn't move. The box remained shut. Rani's face, her voice – the way she'd said, 'Are you missing something, Maryam?', her urgency and her terror – was locked up in that box. I grabbed a sponge from the kitchen and rubbed away the rust around the edges, then prised it open with my nails. A small yellowing sheet of paper, folded over, a single naked piece of paper, not enclosed in an envelope – it hardly seemed worthwhile. A faint smell of dust and metal and the paper sliding around.

Dr Sharma's Private Nursing Home
Grant Road
Dalhousie

I hereby certify that on this day,
17 September, 1968, a female child weighing 8.2 lb.
was born in this hospital at 11.33 am.
Attending doctors; Dr Sharma (obstetrician)
Dr Khwaja (anaesthetist)
Mother, Mrs Rani Roper. Father, Mr Jordan Roper.
No complications. Discharge after five days. Paid
in full.

Signed

N B Sharma

Dr Mrs Nandita B Sharma
17/9/1968

What was this? Rani had a baby? On the same day the Magician had me?

Where was she, my ghost twin?

Thirty-eight

A month before the Magician disappeared, I helped her soak and boil tamarind pods for chutney. The squishy-soft tamarind disintegrated in my fingers as I squeezed out the seeds and set them aside – the little squares made perfect dice. Later, I'd wash them and coax Gloria to play dice with me on the embroidered cloth board Rani Aunty had given us. We loved the game, but the Magician thought it distracted us from homework. She was always telling us to put it away, threatening to confiscate it if she saw us sneaking to the back garden with it. I was getting to be good at the game and Gloria almost always let me win.

The Magician pounded something fragrant with her mortar and pestle. 'What's that smell?' I asked as she emptied a green powder into a small steel bowl and looked around for something, distracted and sweaty.

'Green cardamom. Have you seen my bottle of brahmi? I need it for Rani. I think she has a heart problem – you know, palpitations. A pinch of turmeric mixed with brahmi and cardamom is what she needs.' The Magician pushed her hair off her forehead, leaving a smear of green that I wiped off with the edge of her dupatta. She flinched as if scared. Her agitation was unnerving and I didn't want to be around her.

'Can I wash the seeds now? I don't want to make chutney any more.'

'Oh, Maryam, you're like a frog. You hop from one job to another, finishing nothing. You must learn a little discipline. You are too scattered. Later, when you have a home of your own, you will thank me. Here I am doing three things at the same time and you can't do one?'

'Sorry, Ammi. Of course I'll help. What do you want me to do next?'

We spent the rest of the afternoon together. The Magician worked steadily, pounding and chopping things and piling bowls one on top of the other. She paid no attention to me but would not let me go when I tried to slip away. I sat on a stool and watched her strain the tamarind pulp into a bowl and mix in chilli and sugar and dates. She found her bottle of brahmi and threw a pinch of it into a saucepan of boiled water. She dipped, swirled, whisked and clattered around the kitchen, her distraction increasing by the hour. Something wasn't right. The kitchen was where she loved creating magic – magic with the smells, textures and colours that she spread out on the table, telling us to eat it all or be condemned forever to dry chapattis and watery dal.

'What's the matter, Ammi?'

'Nothing. Why? What's the matter with you?'

'If you're worried about Rani, why don't we take her to a doctor?'

'Don't be silly. There's nothing wrong with Rani. She's as strong as an elephant. Why should we take her to a doctor? And since when have you become so concerned about Rani? Has she said something to you? Or is this another of your stories? Your imagination is going to land us all in trouble one of these days. Don't think I don't know about you hiding in the library with all those books.'

'But —'

'All right, you can go now, Maryam. You've been a good girl. Off you go and find your sister for me.' The Magician held out a samosa dipped in the chutney we'd just finished and offered it to me. I took the samosa and dropped it into a flowerpot outside. She'd forgotten to fry it.

Thirty-nine

The phone rang early one morning, barely ten minutes after Gabriel left, and Jarrah barked sharply. Gloria padded into the kitchen, wrapping a light shawl around her tummy, and raised an eyebrow. It was Clive, his voice croaky and distant. 'Can't explain now but I need you to be ready. Both of you. I'll be at yours in twenty minutes.' He hung up before I could ask any questions.

Gloria and I waited on the verandah, Jarrah lying on her usual chair by the door. Clive arrived in a storm of dust, left the engine running, leaped out and waved at us. I placed my hand in Gloria's and helped her down the steps. She got in the front and I jumped in the back seat, barely closing the door when he was off again.

'The Historian's had a break-in. He's freaking out. Warren's already there. It's pretty bad and he can't handle the old man on his own.' Clive leaned back and patted Gloria's hand. 'You had to see him sometime.'

'Fair enough.' Gloria smiled. She was so much like the Magician these days: unflappable, gentle, beautiful – her mother's daughter.

A police car was parked on the kerb in front of the Historian's house. The front door had a hole where the lock used to be, and the flyscreen leaned against the wall beside the door. Books scattered along the driveway like a memory. The side window smashed. Neighbours on the lawn and a detective pulling on plastic gloves with a grimace.

The Historian turned to look at us when we got out of the car. His unblinking eyes watched Gloria walk slowly towards him and my stomach twisted. He held out his arms. 'Gloria,' he said, and she lowered her head and extended her arms, so the embrace was conducted at arm's length. I tried to step past them but he put his arm around my waist and pulled me to his side, while keeping his other arm around Gloria. We stood rigid beside him until Gloria patted his arm and murmured that we had work to do.

'Yes, yes, yes.' The Historian blinked a few times and turned us around to face the house.

We stepped into the wreckage. The TV unplugged and sitting on a chair in the front room, an empty black wire CD holder, Ikea shelves still sagging from the weight of discarded books, slashed mattresses, broken ceramic dishes – and the Historian's rumbling rage filling us all.

'Just got home and found this. I was up north all week, you know, business deal. What is the use of neighbours if they can't keep an eye on the place? That useless beekeeper next door claims he didn't hear anything. All my medals – and Father's medals – gone. Kitchen is upside down. Bastards emptied all the rice, dal and tea. I will catch them. Then I'll kill them.' The Historian wiped the corners of his mouth and straightened his shoulders.

We looked at each other. Warren shrugged and held his hands out, palms up. The Historian ignored him and picked up a worn blue Bible from a side table. 'Look,' he showed us the stack of fifty-dollar notes inside the hollow book-box. 'That's five thousand I was going to take to the bank tomorrow. Now it's a reward for catching the *haramzadas*.' My brothers winced and the Historian asked, 'So I can't swear in my own house now?'

Gloria looked at him calmly. 'Why don't you go and get changed? We'll tidy up here. Hannah can make some tea and we'll help you sort this out.'

Clive rang insurance and Warren organised the tradesmen. Gloria and I swept up everything after the police had dusted windowsills and shelves and promised they would find the people responsible. The Historian went to the back patio and Gloria followed him. He turned and put his hand on her shoulder, and she bent her head towards his. This time she let him pull her into a gentle embrace. After a couple of minutes she turned sideways and stared out at the overgrown garden before disentangling herself and stepping around the corner, vanishing from my anxious gaze.

A woman arrived in a bright yellow Volkswagen. She had tapered fingernails and round pink lips. She walked into the house holding a large basket filled with strawberries and champagne and two glasses. When she saw us she put down her basket and looked at us quizzically. 'Goodness, who are you all? Where's Gordy? He called me straight away, you know.' She peered through the windows and trotted past us, flinging her arms out towards the Historian. 'Poor Gordy, last thing you need, my pet. I'm here now. What happened? And who are all these people, Gordy?'

'Stop asking silly questions, Sylvie,' the Historian said, his eyes a slit of blue.

Sylvie giggled. 'Such a temper, Gordy,' she said and we feared for her, especially when she rested pink nails on his arm and tilted her head sideways. The Historian shook her off roughly and she turned to us with a smile. 'You must be friends of Gordy's, or are you related to each other? You two look like brothers,' she said gesturing towards Clive and Warren. Gloria emerged from behind the sagging lattice, and Sylvie frowned and raised an eyebrow. 'And who might you be?'

'Sylvie.' The Historian's voice was a snarl, but the woman fluttered her hands at him and flashed a smile, like a deranged beacon. Clive hustled the Historian inside and Gloria indicated I should help her with the clean-up. We had no idea what to do with Sylvie, so we left her standing by herself, smiling at the garden. When we had lived here, the Historian was discreet about

171

the women. Occasionally we would find one of them in the house if we returned unexpectedly, but they were always herded out firmly. The Historian believed in maintaining appearances, even though he knew it had stopped mattering to us a long time ago.

By evening, the house was almost back to normal, with a new flyscreen and a new front door. Inside, everything was swept up, thrown out, straightened and restocked. I put the books back, grieving over the broken spines and torn pages. Two conquistadors were safe with me, the rest irrevocably lost because the Historian had refused to bring them. Still, even these bright shiny books, chosen for their advice on stocks and shares and the small business model, did not deserve to be roughed up like this.

Warren poured out a double scotch for the Historian and sat him down by the window. Clive rang Leanne and went to sit with Warren and the Historian. I took Sylvie by the arm and eased her out the door, she still chattering on about poor Gordy and how lovely it was to meet his family at last. Gloria dozed on the couch, hands laced over her tummy. The questions could wait.

Forty

Gloria ran her finger slowly over the lines and held the journal open on her lap like it was a holy book. She read reverentially, as we had been taught as children, mouth moving soundlessly, pausing over a word she was unsure of, looking into the distance as if remembering something – then – a gasp and she shut the journal. She stood up, turned away from me.

'Gloria?' She looked at me, eyes brimming.

'It doesn't make any sense, Hannah. The Magician must have lost her mind. These are stories, just little fantasy stories with our names as characters. Sad little stories she must have written when she was depressed or something. And the little sketches don't match the stories. Nothing here about…you know…what you found.'

'What have you found?' Clive's quiet voice in the room made us both jump. We hadn't heard him. 'What are you two up to?' He looked at the green journal and the Little Bo Peep tin with the paper still folded over.

I brushed away the doom leaking from Gloria's eyes. 'It's Rani,' I said. 'Poor Rani had a child on the same day I was born. Something must have happened to it – her. It was a girl. That's why Rani went mad. She lost her child. And the Historian tried to protect her.' I handed over the piece of paper – the receipt of a birth, to my brother.

Clive looked at the paper I held open. His face went red and he sat down on the couch where Gloria had been sitting a moment before. He shook his head and dropped it into his large, square hands. 'Oh God, God, God, Christ in Heaven, what are we going to do?'

It shocked me to hear Clive invoke a deity we were ambivalent about. I reached out and he seemed not to notice, ducking his head when my hand touched it. 'Gloria's reading the Magician's journals to see if she knew anything about it. But it's gibberish – if you want, Gloria can read it out loud,' I said to my shaking brother.

'I don't want to hear it. Get away from me – both of you.' Clive rushed from the room before we could say anything else.

'Don't go after him, Hannah. Give him time. This is a lot to take in. Come here – sit with me.' We sat quietly side by side. I tasted bile at the base of my throat and the room swam out of focus. In came the goats with bloody horns in a field of red. The Historian held me high in his arms. The Magician called out to me from behind a silver veil. The hills behind the old house shook and a gap opened up beneath my feet and I fell in, again. *Discharge after five days. Paid in full.*

When I came to, I was lying on the couch with my head on Gloria's lap. Gabriel and Clive looked down at me. Leanne fanned my face with a tea towel.

April, according to the English poet, is the cruellest month. It didn't help that the days were blue with expansive skies and the evenings sharp with flamboyant sunsets. It only made our misery acute.

My strategy was to wear down Gabriel's defences. Especially now that Gloria was living with us. She wore her pregnancy lightly, glowingly. The house had never looked better. Soft cotton quilts appeared over worn couches and fresh flowers sat on corner tables. She straightened frames in the hallway and made the kitchen sparkle. The verandah was swept clear of leaves and the wisteria trimmed back to frame the arch. She insisted we sit down and eat our meals together, made friends with Jarrah and suggested it was time to confront the Historian.

'The truth?' I asked. 'You think he's going to tell us the truth? If he could eliminate the father of this baby by falsifying his name on the birth certificate, what makes you think he's going to tell us anything now?'

Gloria and Gabriel exchanged a look. I knew that look, knew what they were thinking – thinking that awful thing, that I was the baby in the note. That Rani was my mother. Not the Magician.

I shook my head. 'You guys are so transparent. You still think that's me? How is that even possible? I have my own birth certificate, the same as you, Gloria, and Clive and Warren. Come on – how many times have we looked at them?'

Gabriel rubbed the back of his neck and leaned his elbows on the table. Even in this weather he wore a T-shirt over his blue jeans, and I stopped myself from stroking the hair that curled on his forearms. I couldn't think of him like that now. For a while at least. He stood up and stretched, then left us without a word.

'Hannah, this is not your fault. We are all in this together – we all need to know what's going on. And if – I'm saying *if* – the baby is you, don't you want to find Rani? Don't you want to know why the Historian put his name down as the father? Gordon/Jordan? Don't we want to know who Rani really is?'

'What if she is really his sister? And if he really is my father?' My mouth let go of the words reluctantly. 'What sort of a *harami* does that make me?'

Father, Mr Jordan Roper. No complications. Paid in full.

Forty-one

'You know I'm right, Gabriel. If this thing about me is true – and all indications point in that direction – then what I'm saying isn't all that crazy now, is it?' We were in our favourite spot in his garden, where it fell away from raised flowerbeds and meandered down the hill to merge with marri and peppermints. Gloria was asleep somewhere in the house. She fell asleep in the strangest places – in the kitchen, Jarrah's chair by the door, on floor cushions. Catnaps, she called them.

'I can't marry your sister to give her an Australian visa.' Gabriel ran his fingers through his hair and looked at me with that expression he'd acquired as a defence against me – an angry, icy frown that knotted his brows – and spoke with exaggerated slowness. 'You're not being rational. This isn't how it works. I want to help – I truly do. I don't want her to go back to Iran and fend for herself. But – I love you. Does that mean anything to you? I don't care who your father is. Or your mother. Or the fact that you're making it really hard for me to keep loving you.'

I thought about letting it all go, letting what he wanted happen. This was what I grieved over most – his breath, his voice, his anger. The promiscuity of sharing a house if not a life with him. I tasted his words and tried to swallow my own, but I had to remind him of what I'd become. 'Thank you, Gabriel. You can't really mean that. My mother and father – whether you care about it or not – are also brother and sister. And that's not natural. I'm not natural.

If you marry Gloria, you'll have a chance at being normal. You can't deny she's gorgeous.'

'Hannah, drop it, for Christ's sake. What is wrong with you?' Gabriel took long quick steps up to the house and the back door slammed. All our conversations ended the same way these days. I hoped he hadn't woken Gloria.

Winter rains had swept leaves down the hill and banked up woodchips along the path. The earth squelched under my gumboots. A pure blue sky meant it would be a cold day. I stared at the trees and the homeward-bound cockatoos and thought about my brothers' reaction to this new person I had become. Their distaste – the way they flinched – the surreptitious calls when they thought I was at work. And the dreams that no longer tormented me. Only Gloria, because she was the Magician's daughter, still touched me. How long before Gabriel noticed? How long before he understood that monsters like me had no right to men with angel names?

Mother. Father. Paid in full.

Forty-two

Gloria's baby was born in September. All night long a keening wind tugged at trees and rattled the roof. Thunderous rain drummed down on the car as we drove to the hospital and hurried through a streaming car park. Inside, hooded, muffled figures sat on chairs and stared out the windows. The TV showed defeated homes and stranded cars and issued warnings of traffic chaos for office-goers. We settled Gloria into her private room and went outside to wait. She didn't want anyone with her. We'd begged – Leanne and I and Clive. Even Gabriel. She'd said no.

In the morning a watery sun splashed against the windows and fogged my breath. A nurse tapped my arm and gestured that I follow her.

'Just you,' the nurse said as Leanne got up to follow. 'Hannah. You can all see her after. She's fine – and so is the baby.'

Gloria lay on the sterile bed with a tiny white bundle beside her. 'Aunty Hannah, meet your niece, Bahareh. What else can we call her, this spring baby? What do you think?'

The nurse picked up the baby and placed her in my arms. She seemed weightless. I stared at the puckered face forming a yawn, touched a tiny ringlet and smiled at Gloria. 'Bahareh. Of course,' I said. Then Leanne was beside me, and Clive and Warren, and we stood in tight circle, smiling, and Gloria watched us.

∞

We couldn't do enough. In the weeks that followed, Bahareh became the miracle we hadn't expected. She smiled when we peered and crooned at her, and Gloria looked as if she had been in training for this all her life, so gifted was she with instinct and good sense. My brothers and their girlfriends dropped in after work, and the house filled with voices and the clatter of teacups in the kitchen. Gabriel said it was like living in a migrant hostel, but he grinned and winked at me and my heart began the slow beat back to normal. The Historian visited, a little too often. He chuckled over his granddaughter's smallest achievements – a smile, a yawn, a burp. He waved away Gloria's protests that his gifts were too extravagant and bought a new cot, a bassinet, a stroller and a basketful of soft toys. One afternoon he arrived with an elaborate mobile that took Gabriel a few hours to untangle and hook to the ceiling. We stood back to admire it and Bahareh fell asleep. The doting grandfather laughed and paced softly around the room, peering into her cot.

'I'll see you later,' I said to the back of the Historian's head and ran outside to draw deep breaths under the old casuarina. Lately I'd begun to have trouble breathing around the Historian. Gabriel thought I might be having panic attacks. He offered to come with me to see the doctor. I told him what I told Gloria. 'I'm fine. I really am. I'm just allergic to the Historian.'

I hereby certify that on this day, a female child thought about plunging a knife into her father's heart. No complications. Paid in full.

I didn't need to worry about Gloria going back to India or, worse, to Sohrab in Iran. She didn't want to. And the Historian wasn't about to let his daughter out of his sight after she'd given him his first grandchild. A sponsorship was produced, support affidavits were signed, and Gloria and her baby became resident Australians. Gabriel cocked an ironic brow and sat with us on the verandah in the evenings, his eyes daring mine to meet his.

Gloria hand-stitched a quilt using small squares of material I thought I recognised. I sat with a book of Matthew Arnold's poems on my lap and tried to remember what the Magician looked like. Importantly, what did she look like now? Was her body still soft under the summer kaftans she sometimes wore? Did she make that gurgling sound when she sipped her tea? Did she smell of cinnamon and saffron still? Did she think about us? When had she found out about me – the monster in her nest?

Once, when I was chosen to run in the relay at our annual sports day, the Magician promised she would come to see me run. I ran so hard my chest hurt and my lips bled, and my team won. I went home with a little silver cup and saw the Magician in her usual spot in the garden, her back to the sun, sketchpad on her knees. She smoothed my hair down when I leaned into her embrace.

'You forgot. You didn't come. You promised.'

'What did I forget? What's that in your hand?'

'It's a cup. Because I came first.'

'Your race? Was that today? Maryam, I thought it was next week, my darling, clever girl – show me that cup.' The Magician kissed the cup I held out, hugged me and hustled me away indoors. She made sweet milky tea and sat me down on a kitchen stool while I sipped, murmured an apology for missing my moment of sporting glory and said she would make it up to me. 'We'll have a special day – you and me – we'll go out and do something nice. Okay?'

'Ammi, I know you're busy. You can come next year.'

'You're a good girl, Maryam. And I'm a forgetful mother.'

I didn't run in the relay again, preferring the society of table tennis and badminton over long hours running around the oval by myself. The Magician never came to a school event for me. Gloria comforted me – I mustn't mind, she said; the Magician was worn out with the effort of remembering what we did at different times.

So worn out that she didn't know she was a grandmother now.

Forty-three

The Historian said he would have Bahareh's first birthday party at home – his home, not ours, the home my brothers and I had left as soon as we could. He talked about it for months and asked us what we thought. Pink balloons or pink-and-white balloons? Family only or family and friends? Indian food or Australian food?

Our brothers were told to hire chairs and cutlery and buy champagne. Gloria was not to do anything – she and Bahareh were guests of honour.

Aunty Frankie said it was a good thing Gloria was such a sensible mum. 'That child won't ever need to lift a finger. She just has to look at your dad with her big brown eyes and he'll pluck his heart out and lay it at her feet.'

The thought of Sohrab hovered between us as Gloria and I dressed Bahareh in her frilly princess frock. She never mentioned him but I saw the shadows on her face and knew she felt the guilt. As I did.

At the house, the Historian rocked back and forth on his heels impatiently, holding his arms out for his favourite girl. He laughed and clapped when Bahareh reached out towards him. 'What more can a grandfather ask for, eh? Come in – come, come quickly, all of you. I have something to tell you on this happy occasion.' He lifted Bahareh from her stroller and handed her a pink balloon.

It was family only after all. Aunty Frankie and Uncle Steve. Their daughters. My brothers and their girlfriends. And Gabriel.

No Sylvie, though. The Historian had always had a flair for drama and now he stood with Bahareh in his arms and twirled around with her. She squealed and he laughed. 'Happy Birthday, precious girl, welcome to your new home. Yes, that's right, this is your present. I have signed the deeds over to you, and your mother can look after it for you until you are old enough.'

He looked at us, smile slipping a little. 'Well, what do you think? Seeing as none of you are interested, what am I going to do with it? This was always meant to be a family home, not something for me to rattle around in – alone. And Gloria needs somewhere more permanent. She can't go on moving from pillar to post. This is ideal, don't you think?'

Gloria threaded her fingers through her hair and looked at us. We shook our heads. We knew nothing.

'Well?' the Historian asked. 'Is anyone going to speak? I want my daughter and granddaughter safe and secure in their own house – how can you argue with that?'

'I don't need your house, Dad. I'm quite happy with my current arrangements.' Gloria looked distracted, as if she wanted to cry.

'This is the trouble with young people these days. No foresight. You don't look beyond your current arrangements. You have a child to think about now. You need to plan. Come, let me show you something, and after you've seen it you can make up your mind, eh?' The Historian marched off towards the back of the house, where the bedrooms were. We followed him to the room that had been mine.

When we lived here, my brothers and I, we lived as itinerants, refusing to claim the space as ours in protest at having been uprooted. No posters on the walls, no magazines on the floor, no music in the hallway. We slept on the beds and placed our clothes inside the wardrobes. We chose nothing and asked for nothing. If we found perfume and make-up in the bathroom or earrings and champagne flutes on the coffee table, we didn't question their appearance, just as we didn't question the women who came and went with the Historian in the house he was determined to call 'ours'. For three years we circulated around the shared space like polite strangers, and when we left, we left entirely.

What we saw now was a sparkling new space – a nursery with pale pink walls and heritage quilts over a hand-carved cot. A bedroom a baby would grow into, leading to a larger bedroom for Gloria, an enormous bathroom with a change room, and windows looking out at freshly planted gardens with wisteria and grapevines and buffalo grass. More Magician, less Historian.

'Say yes,' I whispered to Gloria. 'You deserve this.'

The Historian held out his arms and Gloria lowered her head and walked towards him.

Aunty Frankie tapped her on the back and said, 'I'm so pleased you like it. I had such fun putting it together. He's all right, your old man. Deep pockets and a big heart.'

Forty-four

I drove Gloria to Point Walter, where the river meets parkland and open bush. There had been a migrant hostel here until the early seventies. Gabriel and his parents had lived in it briefly, the last of the ten-pound Poms. 'A plasterboard bedroom with two beds and a dining hall with tables that seated six,' was how his mother described it. 'Mum and Dad and little Gabriel, fresh off the boat and straight into a West Australian summer with flies and heat and everything.'

I followed the road past the casuarinas and marri and banksias, and told Gloria about the long sand spit I had once walked on, at low tide, terrified I would be marooned there, a non-swimmer's fear.

'I'd be scared too,' Gloria said. 'But don't change the subject. I still don't know why you're driving me around like you're my mother. I told you it would be easier if I caught the bus.'

'And I told you I'm not letting you walk blindly into volunteering for something that might be dodgy. All we know about this guy is he's some sort of philanthropist who runs programs for refugees out of his garage. He could be a psycho.'

'And you're such a fine judge of character,' Gloria smiled.

I pulled up outside the address we'd been given on the phone. A blond-brick driveway led to the white stucco mansion. There was space enough for six cars and I slid in under a weeping willow. A few children were running around the garden, watched over by a woman who waved at us.

Bahareh sat upright in her car seat, clutching a Cabbage Patch doll, giggling when Gloria opened the back door to chuck her under the chin. I hoped she would make a fuss and cry when she saw her mother disappear into the house, obliging Gloria to abandon this crazy idea. But Bahareh came from a long line of placid, determined women, and reached her dimpled arms towards her mother when she bent down to kiss her.

'Be a good girl for *masi* today.' Gloria stroked her daughter's cheek with the back of her fingers.

'Marcie,' repeated Bahareh with a grin. 'Mummy Marcie.'

'That's right darling. Mummy's busy and *masi* will look after you today. Won't you, Hannah?' Gloria looked at me and I lowered my eyes and patted her arm.

'Of course. Come on, Little Miss Muffet, let's go and have some fun.'

'Fun,' said Bahareh as Gloria waved us away.

I was late. Bahareh had fallen asleep after a couple of hours at the park and I had to wake her. She grizzled and cried as I strapped her into the seat with a bottle of juice and a biscuit. When I got to the house at Point Walter, I scooped up Bahareh along with the doll, the bottle and the soggy biscuit, and looked around. Gloria waved from the front of the house and signalled that we should walk up.

'Mummy,' Bahareh wailed and tried to pitch out of my arms. 'Marcie Mummy.'

'Hello, princess,' Gloria said as we arrived, panting. 'You look sleepy,' she said to the child straining towards her and took her from me. A woman with a heart-shaped face under a printed silk scarf turned towards us as Bahareh lifted a sticky finger and pointed at her.

A familiar face. A face that used to dimple easily into a smile. A face that had lain next to mine on a bed for thirty-seven nights.

'*Salaam*, Hannah,' she said.

185

Roya. Beautiful, vanilla-scented Roya, who had been snatched away at midnight by revolutionary men, stood under the shade of a river red gum and kissed my cheek. Her lips were dry and when the scarf slipped I saw it; the long thin red line that extended from her hairline down the side of her face almost to her jaw. She drew back at the look on my face and burst into tears. 'Oh, Hannah, I am so glad to see you. You are safe, both of you are safe, and my heart is happy to see that. I am so sorry for this, *azizam*, but I have bad news. Sohrab *jun* is no more,' she sobbed, and Gloria placed her hands over her daughter's ears.

That night, after tucking a sleepy Bahareh into her baby seat, we drove again to the river – this time where it curves around the bend at Mounts Bay Road. It was calm and quiet ripples silvered its surface. Kings Park loomed behind us and a dwindling moon made leaf patterns dance on the path in front of us. A scent of crushed peppermint and grass mingled with the whiff of charred meat from someone's barbecue.

Gabriel and I walked with hunched shoulders, heads down. Gloria carried Bahareh in her arms and Roya kept pace beside her. We moved off the path to accommodate a swift cyclist in Lycra, and stepped into wet grass near the river's edge.

Gloria withdrew a crushed yellow rose from her shoulder bag and scattered the petals into the river. She stroked her sleeping daughter's face and recited a line from that wretched poem of which the Magician was so fond – '*And I will tell thee what my heart desires – the dead need no one, claim no kin.*'

Forty-five

On the surface, it wasn't so bad. Gabriel and I accommodated each other easily enough and contained our miseries in daily rituals. We made love, went to work, bought things, met people and took turns walking Jarrah. Sometimes brief parcels of those moments were hard to bear. Like when Gabriel detached from the messiness of my life so completely I was freshly orphaned. Or when I heard him on the phone to someone, laughing with his head flung back, knowing that deep-throated concern was for someone else. A letter arrived from Japan and he tucked it into the pocket over his heart without looking at me.

'Get out of my kitchen.' Gabriel prodded Jarrah with his toe one evening when I simmered rice in a pot, ready to add to the chicken – a pale version of the Magician's biryani.

'It's her kitchen too,' I said. Jarrah stood up and stretched before sliding under the kitchen table and thumping her tail on Gabriel's foot.

'Hannah? Put that down and sit for a minute. We need to talk.' That look in his eyes. Measuring, weighing, distancing. I rushed into the void.

'I'm sorry, Gabriel. I've been an idiot.'

'That you have.'

'I'm trying to apologise.'

'Go on, then. I'm listening.'

I shrugged and spread my hands out, looking at Gabriel, his unreadable face, and forced the words out before resolve failed again. 'I'm going to India. I need to find the Magician and Rani.'

'I thought you might say that. I'm coming with you.'

'Really?'

'Really. Try and stop me. You're a stubborn woman, but you're still my stubborn woman.' Gabriel's eyes met mine, completely.

Gloria put Bahareh down on the rug beside her feet and looked up. Gabriel bent down and picked up the child. 'I'll leave you two alone,' he said. 'Don't be too long, and for heaven's sake, Gloria, don't try and make her change her mind.' He strode outside with Bahareh's arms clasped firmly around his neck.

'Shame, Hannah, shame.' Gloria's voice was low.

'What are you on about?'

'You —' Gloria said, cheeks tinged pink. 'I thought I knew my baby sister. I thought I could trust her judgement. Trust her not to humiliate me. How could you? Did you imagine I wouldn't find out?'

Oh, no. She knew.

'Gloria, it made sense at the time. I know it sounds crazy now — but I didn't want to lose you and I thought —'

'You thought it was okay to ask your boyfriend to marry your married sister. Not cool, Hannah, not cool at all.' Gloria folded baby clothes into squares and looked at me. Sohrab's ghost shivered between us. It was the second time I had betrayed them and it seemed as if this time it would be as catastrophic as the first. I was losing her again.

After a moment's silence, Gloria looked at me. 'Is there something wrong with me? My daughter's father is dead and all I feel is relief. I loved him, you know. I followed him into a revolution and kept him alive when he didn't want to live, to see. I learned to speak his language and love his mother when I had no idea where mine was. All that, and he goes and dies anyway. What was the point?'

I put my arms around her. She sighed and hugged me. I breathed in baby oil and honey and smoothed her long hair down her back. Brushing the back of her fingers against my cheek, she leaned back in my embrace, blinking and averting her gaze.

'Darling Hannah. I wish you weren't so bloody-minded. I wish I'd stayed to look after you. This isn't fair – this horrible family secret that's making you act like a crazy person. Thank goodness Gabriel's going with you. Here's Marina's address. You remember Mrs D'Silva's daughter? I stayed with her when I ran away and she's probably still there. People don't move around much in India, do they? Anyway, if she's not there, someone in the building will tell you where she is. *Khuda Hafiz.* Come back soon. And if you find them, Ammi and Rani, bring them back with you.'

After dinner that night, Gabriel stretched out on the couch and listened quietly while I berated myself for hurting Gloria, for what I'd asked him to do, for being a twit. He watched me pace up and down, reached out and drew me down against the length of his body. I listened to his heart and breathed in his kiss. 'I told her,' he said. 'I had to – you wouldn't give up.'

'Gabriel – how could you? She's devastated. Wait…when did you tell her?' I pulled away from him and sat on the edge of the couch.

'A few months ago.' Gabriel took my cold hands in both of his and rubbed them. 'She was outraged, all right. She waved her hands about and called you names in three different languages. She apologised for not raising you properly. Then she calmed down and said she would teach you a lesson. That was the lesson.'

'She heaped shame on me – she pulled a Magician on me. I wanted to crawl out of there on my belly. She called me a crazy person.'

'You are a crazy person.'

'Gabriel.'

'Do you solemnly swear never to farm me out to your relatives?' Gabriel's hands warmed my back and he drew me to him again.

'I swear by all the conquistadors of India,' I said to his chest, listening to our hearts thump unevenly against each other.

Part IV

Home

The Magician makes sure we have starched school uniforms, nit-free heads, brown-paper-covered books, hand-knitted red cardigans and short nails. She feeds us all, several times a day, bestowing salted nuts and sweetened milk as treats upon us on cold nights. When the lost boy arrives to share our lives, she tells us it is God's way of reminding us we have much to be thankful for. We thank Him for each other and for her, and she makes us thank Him for the others. It is hard to be thankful for a captive aunt and a thunderous father but we try.

She doesn't belong here – in this brown dusty town where the wind whistles and snaps the sad trees in half. She looks as if she misses something she cannot remember – snow on a mountain and a blue-domed mosque and a man and a woman with eyes like hers.

Forty-six

India was on the verge of another crisis, with Rajiv Gandhi freshly killed and Mumbai in the grip of communal riots. We checked into a hotel near the airport and took a cab to the address Gloria had scribbled on a Post-It note.

Mrs D'Silva's daughter looked exactly as I remembered her, a small, neat woman with curly black hair and a short-sighted squint. She had never married. Her flat was crammed with soft toys on every available surface. I kept my bag on my lap and shared the couch with a large brown bear wearing a bow tie. Gabriel moved aside a smaller bear and sat on a straight-backed plastic chair. Marina kissed me on both cheeks, wiped her eyes and blew her nose into a little pink hanky. I murmured my regrets on her mother's passing.

'She lived a good life,' Marina said. 'In a way, I'm glad she didn't live to see this. What to tell you, Hannah? This used to be my city. I don't know it any more. We hear about bombs going off and drug lords doing something and blaming it on the Hindus – my poor mother would have been so scared. But you look the same, you know. She would have loved to see you. You were always her favourite, my girl.' Marina poured thick milky tea in little green cups and urged us to eat *chaklis* and *bhajias*. I remembered her mother's cupcakes and coloured wool and sensed the Magician's presence.

'Marina,' I said. 'Thank you for seeing us. I know it's a bit unexpected, us on your doorstep like this, but Gloria said you'd help.'

Marina nodded several times and busied her hands with plates and saucers. She spooned careful heaps of yellow halva onto two mismatched plates and offered them to us.

'So, do you know where they are? Rani and Mrs Roper?' Gabriel leaned forward and Marina's hands wobbled as she placed the plates in front of us.

'Only one person knows for sure. That Meher. And she won't tell anyone. My poor mother went to her grave asking for them – but no, that creature would not tell. I can take you to her house, not far from here. But whether or not she tells you – that's for you to find out.' Marina shook her head and wiped her mouth, pushing another plate of food towards us.

A slow breeze lifted a curtain by the window, and I dabbed at my face with a tissue. The open windows circulated steamy Mumbai smells and sounds: samosas, sweat, flowers, rot, car horns, shouts. It was always hot here. Hot and noisy. The aunties used to tell us how peaceful it was to be away from the teeming city, away from its neon-lit insomnia, its cacophony. Meher was here, somewhere. She was the price I had to pay to find my mothers.

A scooter rickshaw waited outside Marina's tiny flat and we got in, Gabriel incredulous that we were all going to squeeze into it. With a whine we took off along lanes and potholed streets, pumping fumes and heat. Cars, buses, shops and animals flashed past in a blur until the neighbourhood changed and the streets became wider, quieter and tree-lined.

'Posh part of town,' Gabriel said softly, and I nodded. This was Pali Hill in Bandra, abode of film stars and Bollywood identities. How could Meher afford to live here? When she'd lived with us she had nothing. The Magician said we would be paid a hundredfold if we looked after those less fortunate than us, especially family.

Outside a heavy door with the name Meher Mohsen painted in black below a peephole, I rang the bell and waited for my heart to stop jumping. An instant clatter of footsteps and a voice yelled: '*Kaun hai*? Who is it?'

'It's Maryam. I'm here to see Meher Aunty. I have a message from Gordon Roper.'

The footsteps receded and the house went quiet. After five minutes I rang the bell again. Gabriel thumped on the door and I kept my finger on the bell, hearing it shrill inside like an alarm. Marina joined us – knocking on the door along with Gabriel and calling out. A man from the flat behind us opened his door and shook his head. We ignored him. For an hour we stood there, shouting, thumping, ringing – then a woman wearing a white dupatta over her hennaed hair flung open the door and stood aside, pointing inwards.

A gloomy corridor led to a tepid room with a balcony that overlooked a park. Meher, still large, sat here in a wheelchair wearing a paisley-print kaftan and a squint of rage. There was no evidence of anyone else in the flat. The servant who had let us in slunk away and Meher glared at her receding back.

'So, why have you come to harass your poor old aunty this time, eh?' Her voice was as strong as ever and her hands dismissed Marina and Gabriel in an instant.

'Tell me where my mother is. I'm not going anywhere until you do.' My voice emerged, surprising me.

'What mother? As if *haramis* have the right to ask,' Meher said loudly, emphasising the words. 'No right at all.' Beside me Marina sucked in her breath and held my hand.

'Look at you, Meher,' I said. 'Still angry. Abuse me all you like, but you're going to tell me where my mother and aunt are.'

The maid emerged from the kitchen and stared at us. I pressed a hundred-rupee note into her hand and told her to go out for a while. She tucked the note into her bra and went out, shutting the door behind her.

Meher blinked, venom clouding her eyes. I held her gaze. 'Where's my mother? Where's Rani? What do you know? Come on, you're old now – and you hate me so much, you might as well tell me why.'

Gabriel put his arm around my waist and drew me to his side. Marina murmured a Hail Mary.

'Farah is not your mother. That half-breed darkie is. Rani. There. Go now. You know.' Meher raised her voice and her arm at the same time and I flinched, even though she hadn't moved from her spot.

'Where are they?' Gabriel's voice was quiet and Meher ignored him. To me he said, 'Offer her some money. You said she was always greedy. Make her an offer.' This was a side to Gabriel I hadn't encountered before, his voice low with contempt and rage. I pressed his hand and nodded. Then I stepped up to the wheelchair where Meher sat wedged and looked down at her.

'Where are they? How much do you want? Look, I've got lots of money and time.' I tapped the money belt around my waist and unzipped it a fraction to show her the new 500-rupee notes with bank staples holding them together. Meher stared back with such intensity that Marina pulled me back and whispered that even the devil was more compassionate.

'You think you can buy me, little girl? You, with your fancy man and your half-breed friend? You think you can give me more than all this?' Meher waved her arm to indicate the flat. 'Thanks to that man you call your father, as you can see, I'm well provided for. Save your taxi money and go away now.'

'We're not going anywhere. And your maid isn't coming back either.' Gabriel folded his arms over his chest and walked to the couch facing the balcony, with the air of someone in no hurry to be elsewhere. Marina sat down next to him and I leaned back against the wall.

'Go away, all of you. Harassing a poor old woman like this. You can't just sit there. What have you done to my servant? I need to go to the bathroom. I have to take my medicine. I will die if I don't eat at the correct time.'

'Too bad, Meher Aunty.' I kept my voice even. 'Where's my mother?'

Meher beat her chest with a fist and wailed. She scrunched her face and wept, and I remembered how quickly the aunties could switch from laughter to sorrow and back again. I tried to hold the Magician's face in my mind and steeled myself against the noise made by the wobbling woman in front of me. Gabriel watched me, his body poised to spring back beside me in an instant.

Meher closed her mouth and moved her hand away from her face. She was moist with exertion but dry-eyed. 'Shimla,' she said. 'They are in Shimla. I promised them I would never tell that man, so now it is on your head. If that *goonda* ever finds them, it'll be your fault. My conscience is clear. I can go to my Maker with a clear heart.'

'Thank you.' Gabriel's shadow loomed on the evening wall beside us and he reached for my hand and drew me to his side. I sagged towards him and laced my fingers through his.

Meher said to me in Urdu, 'He knows you're a *harami* and he still touches you?'

'I need an address —'

'Dalhousie,' Meher said. The words rushed out of her now. She wiped the corners of her mouth, tugging at the beaded gold necklace around her neck. 'That's where you were born. I was there. With Rani and your father. Farah came later. We told her what Rani had done and she agreed to raise you with her own. We said Rani had run away with a married man and we had to rescue her. So many lies — we told so many lies. Saint, that woman — no one else would have done what my Farah did. That is class and breeding. *We* have class and good breeding. My Farah picked up the filthy rubbish that came out of that darkie and took it home. Took you home. Never said a word. Raised you as her own.'

'And my father? Who is he?'

'Oh, ho. Gordon, of course. Who else? *Chee chee.*' Meher slapped her cheeks with her hands and stared at us. 'That's why we could never tell Farah. Brother, sister. *Toba, toba.* And not the first time, either. Been doing it since they were children. That's what he said to me — your *father* — when he told me to keep quiet, when I walked into the room one time. He was doing it again with her. And she just let him. How convenient for her to be locked up, called a *pagli*. Isn't it better to die than do this thing – this *paap*? Look at you – you're not natural. God never intended for this to happen. How can you call him your father – this monster? He paid for this flat – with his *haram ki kamai*. How else could I live here in my old age with no one to look after me but that lazy servant? At least the money makes her stay.' She stopped to draw in her breath and picked her nose.

And there it was – the wretched story of my birth – flung at me like acid while Gabriel and Marina looked down at their feet.

'An address,' I repeated. 'Where in Shimla are they?'

Forty-seven

The Magician disappeared on the last day of her prayer vigil for Sohrab. That's what confused us initially – we thought it had something to do with Sohrab. Something to do with the wretchedness of his orphaned status – his slaughtered family, his broken country. Of course it wasn't that at all. The Magician left us because she found out the Historian was sleeping with his sister. My heartbroken Magician. As always, she protected the most vulnerable, and no one can deny that poor, captive Rani was vulnerable. My brothers were supposed to look after us, meanwhile, and they would come back for us when they could. Yes, that was what she had planned to do – not abandon us, not leave us to our own devices and the Historian's far-from-tender mercies. When they were safe. But the Historian's trump card – Australia – was not one the Magician had seen coming, so how could she know what would happen when she left with Rani?

'Don't fuss, Farah,' I remember Rani saying when we visited her in the attic on *that* morning. 'Look after your children first. I can manage.'

'My children are strong. They can manage very well without me. You can't. And it is my honour to look after you.'

The Magician was beautiful that day. She wore a silk sari in swirling shades of purple because she was going to the movies with one of the aunties. 'I wish I could take you out, Rani. It's not fair – you stuck here like this.'

'Enjoy yourself and don't worry about me.' Rani turned away quickly and busied herself with a tablecloth she was embroidering. I didn't like the colours she used – bold pinks and yellows that looked wrong against the brown cotton.

'Why can't we take her out when the Historian is away?' I tugged at the Magician's hand as we walked away from the locked door. 'We can send the servants away too and no one will know.'

'He'll know,' the Magician said tiredly. 'He always knows. No, we can't take that chance. I can't fail in my duty.'

When the Magician returned from her movie she went straight to the attic. She came back too quickly and said she had a headache. She stayed in her room for the rest of the evening. Gloria and the aunties served dinner and the Historian pushed his food around. He cracked his knuckles and twisted his ring round and round on his little finger. He didn't seem bothered that Warren and Clive arrived late and complained about the food being cold. Outside, the night was black and a dry wind picked up dust and small stones and flung them against the barred windows. No one remembered to switch on the outside light. Gloria prodded me to finish dinner and told me she would sleep with me. I was not to bother the Magician. We read stories from *A Thousand and One Nights* and fell asleep in each other's arms.

In the morning the Magician was gone. So was Rani.

Forty-eight

'I can't,' I said. 'I don't think I can look at them. I know I said I wanted to find them, but…I don't want to see them any more. I don't trust myself and I don't understand why someone who's supposed to love us and look after us would abandon us like that. Why did they leave us with that man if —?'

Gabriel turned from the circular window of our room at Hotel Imperial and said, 'That's snow there – right? Over there, just over the ridge – that is actual snow and those are the Himalayas?'

'Gabriel.'

'Yes. We're doing this together, Hannah, and then we're going home. We're here because this is important, because you know you need to do this. And I've never seen snow on the Himalayas before.'

'What will I call them? Which one shall I call Ammi? I suppose the Magician isn't related to me at all. She's nothing. Nothing but a liar who left us.'

'Hannah.' Gabriel pulled me towards him and I squashed my face into his chest and the slow beat of his heart, into his skin, his untainted skin.

∞

We climbed a stone staircase with iron handrails painted red and stood outside a brown door for a minute to catch our breath. Behind us, the road twisted around into a valley thick with banyan, pine and chinar, limbs and roots swaying in the mist. Every terraced house on this winding street clung to the side of a hill so steep it seemed impossible the houses didn't tumble down like the stones that had slithered past us when we cut through the woods to get here. This was the summer capital of the British in India, I remembered. Grandfather William had been stationed here and had hated the faux Englishness, the Gothic spires, the Victorian women; he couldn't wait to return to the soft dusty plains.

Eleven years. I was fourteen when I had last seen them. I lifted the brass knocker and tapped it a few times, thrusting my hands deep into the sheepskin jacket I had never worn in Perth. I had never been this cold before.

The door opened slowly and it was dark behind the woman who peered out at us. She stepped out on the landing and the sky turned grey, like her eyes, her hair. The Magician. At last. Weathered and uncomprehending. A frown on her face.

'Ammi. How are you?'

Gabriel stepped around me and stood beside the Magician. She stared at me and put both hands out, like a blind woman. I took her hand in mine and stroked her wet cheek.

'Maryam? My Maryam?'

'Ammi, is my mother here?'

'Come in, both of you – it's going to rain.' And it did – with a boom of thunder and a crash of lightning as we stepped into the house.

Inside, a smell of cinnamon and lavender. In the corner, a jug filled with orange blossoms and beside it on a tall table smoke from a clutch of incense sticks drifting down. Flowers and spice, essential Magician smells. The house with flickering lights and pale walls. Rain falling steadily and thunder crashing in the hills outside.

I took one hand out of my pocket and reached for Gabriel's warm one. 'Rani Aunty? Where is she? How is she? Oh, Ammi, I wish...'

The Magician stretched both arms towards me and I walked into her embrace. I was about ten centimetres taller than her now and didn't know how to fit my body around hers. We stood holding each other like acquaintances at a party, shuffling our feet and murmuring awkwardly. I shut my eyes and tried to remember how we used to do this, tried to sniff her scent, but all I felt was unease.

The Magician stroked my hair briefly and stepped back. 'Sit there,' she said, pointing at a divan layered with quilts and cushions. 'It's the most comfortable seat in the house. Shall I make tea?' A streak of lightning flooded the room with blue and I saw her face clearly, her cheeks still wet, eyes turned away from us.

'Ammi, this is Gabriel. He's come with me from Australia. We wanted to find you and Rani.'

The Magician nodded and waved her hand in the direction of the quilted divan. 'Sit. I'll make tea. Then we'll talk. The lights may go out soon and who knows when...'

We sat down on the divan and held hands. I listened to the thump of my heart and wished I could feel something. I should cry. I should clutch her by the arms and demand answers. I should be devastated, ecstatic, overwhelmed. Gabriel's large hand closed over mine and I sagged towards him.

The Magician walked out of the room, switching on a lamp by the door as she left. It lit up a photograph on the table – a studio portrait of two women in saris smiling at the photographer. Rani and the Magician. I walked across and studied it, lifting the heavy frame and turning it over before placing it back on the table. Rani's dark-lashed eyes that gave nothing away, pointy chin, long hair streaked with grey, and the Magician beside her with tired eyes and pleated lips stretching in a half-smile.

'She looks like you,' Gabriel was beside me. 'The Magician looks like you, I mean.'

'Liar.'

'No, it's true. Haven't you ever heard of nature versus nurture? Fox cubs raised by goats and all that. Physiological characteristics depend more on who raises you than who gives birth to you. That's why couples who live with each other for sixty years look so similar. There's hope for me yet.'

'I love what you're trying to do, Gabriel, even if it's unlikely that my eyes will turn green and my hair blond after sixty years with you.'

'Why would you want to? I was going for a healthy tan and big brown eyes.'

The Magician came in, filling the room with a whiff of cardamom and ginger as she set the tray down in front of us. Some rituals never changed. The room became brighter as the storm died down and a brisk wind cleared the clouds. The valley that had disappeared in sleet and mist swung back into view, and we saw each other's faces clearly.

'Eleven years and two months.' The Magician twisted the edge of her dupatta into a little rope and her voice trembled. 'You're twenty-five years old and I thought I would never see you again. I've lost everything.'

'Ammi, I'm sorry it took so long.' *If you hadn't bloody buggered off, it might have been so different. And you've lost everything? What about me?*

The Magician held out her arms and said, 'Yes, I know. Just as well I have a strong heart. Otherwise it would have stopped a long time ago. Let me look at you properly, Maryam. Come.'

I allowed myself to be folded into another embrace and held myself still within it. After a minute, she stepped back and clasped her hands around mine. 'Have you got any photos? How are the boys? What about Gloria? Any of them married? Children? Ah, for a mother to not know…I'm sorry, my *jaan*…'

'Of course. Where's Rani Aunty? Maybe we can show them to her as well?' I swung around and indicated my handbag, stepping away from her insistent hands. Gabriel held my bag out towards me, eyes thoughtful.

I pulled out the white envelope and sat back down on the divan, Gabriel moving to make room for the Magician. She appeared not to have heard my request for Rani and picked up each photo and passed her fingers over it, exclaiming over Gloria and Bahareh and Warren and Clive, wiping her eyes with the edge of her dupatta. I showed her a picture of Jarrah reclining under the casuarina and she startled me by saying, 'What a beautiful dog. We had one when we first came here. A lovely German shepherd called Matthias. Poor Rani was a little scared at first – but he was a gentle, beautiful dog. Very protective. Went with us everywhere and slept there – on that chair. Oh, the amount of hair I used to sweep up; but, no matter, he's gone now.'

The Magician had not shown the slightest interest in animals when we were little. We begged in vain for cats, dogs, birds and monkeys, but the closest we came to having pets were the turtles in the pond, and they, as Gloria said, didn't do anything. And here she was now, the fastidious Magician, never without a duster, eulogising a large hairy dog. We sat quietly as she went over each photo, shaking her head, wiping her eyes and reaching out to touch my arm occasionally. She even patted Gabriel's hand, pointing him out in a picture of Bahareh's first birthday.

'And Sohrab?' The Magician gripped my arm. 'Where is Sohrab? Why isn't he with his family – with Gloria and Bahareh? You know, I always thought you and Sohrab were more compatible, Maryam. Remember how he couldn't even talk to Gloria? Who would have thought? But look at you, happy now, aren't you? Yes, you and Gabriel make a good couple. What is in our destiny cannot be denied.'

'I'm sorry, Ammi. Sohrab is dead. He died in Iran, with his baba and maman beside him. He was very sick. He went blind and he had a weak heart. I went to Iran to bring Gloria back to Perth but things started to get a little crazy. We had to run away without telling Sohrab. After we escaped, we had no way of keeping in touch. His cousin Roya, who also lives in Perth now, told us what happened. Roya escaped like we did but she had to live in a refugee camp in Pakistan. It was horrible. Ammi, why...'

The Magician took her arm away from mine, covered her face with her dupatta and wept. She made long, keening sounds I'd never heard before. She used to stop the tears before they took hold. We would see her face change, her head go up, her throat move, her eyes shine. No one ever saw her tears and no one doubted that she shed them when we weren't looking. The sounds that came from her now were like the howl of a wolf parted from her cub. Gabriel jumped up from his seat and walked to the window. I stood up too and placed my hands on her shaking shoulders, patting her bent head, wondering where Rani was.

'Maryam.' The Magician's head lifted towards mine and I saw the rumpled face, unguarded.

'Ammi, what is it?'

'You are too late, my child. Rani died last month – not forty days yet.' The Magician's shoulders stopped shaking and she blew her nose into a man's white hanky. 'Like Sohrab, she was sick. Dying. She refused treatment – that is why I brought her here. At least she could live the rest of her life without fear.'

Two quick strides and Gabriel was beside me, an arm around my waist, pulling me into his embrace. The Magician looked at us both and wiped away the tear that trickled down the corner of her left eye. 'I'm sorry. So sorry. But I promised her.'

'What did you promise, Ammi?'

'That you would never find out. It was better you thought I had walked out because – because of your father. She never wanted anyone to make a fuss, never wanted anyone to grieve. She made me promise not to grieve. She was a good woman.'

'She was my mother.'

'Yes – but how...?'

I pulled out the folded piece of paper I carried everywhere with me. 'She gave me this when I was seven years old. She must have known I would look at it. She always intended me to know.'

The Magician reached for a pair of spectacles in a hand-crocheted case. She put them on and peered at the receipt I held. She read it and looked at me, at the paper, at me again, then put it down on the table in front of her. Her hand formed a fist that she placed on her chest. She blinked. 'I don't understand. What is this? Where? This is not right. A horrible mistake. Not Rani.'

I knelt on the floor beside her. 'You really never knew?' I asked as she shuddered and leaned sideways into me, a dead weight.

'A married man. A foreigner who just left her after – you know.' The Magician shook her head vigorously. 'It was a big scandal and we needed to protect you. We agreed. Even your father. Oh, he was furious, and I had to beg him to allow her to come back with us. He was going to send her to the nuns. But you were always coming home with us. Children make their own destiny. Adults make mistakes. I don't know what this is. Maryam – this is nothing to do with you, this wicked piece of paper. I don't know why she would give this to you. Her mind was affected, after all. I'm sorry you thought…My poor child…'

'Ammi.'

'No. No. You are wrong to even think this. Your father is not a saint but he would never do this. And Rani knew the sacrifice I made. She would never deceive me like this. My whole life – I spent my whole life in service to her. She suffered. I suffered with her. She could not do this thing. I gave up my children for her.' The Magician slumped forward, head in hands, the way Clive had, when he had found out. My mother, so good with strays who needed food and warmth, so bad at intuiting accidents of birth. My mother, the only one I had now. I stroked her arm the way she used to stroke mine, a piece of paper between us, despair rising like a river about to burst its banks.

'Ammi, think about it. Why would Rani make up something like this? And isn't this where I was born? You told me about

Dalhousie and how it was the only time you and I were together. It checks out. This doctor still has a clinic, a private clinic there.'

'Yes, yes.' The Magician sounded impatient. She smoothed out the creases in her kameez and nodded as she remembered. 'Of course this is where you were born, and I remember the doctor. But the name is false. Rani is – was – your mother, but putting her own brother's name down as father is wicked, and she has done a very wrong thing. Very wrong. We will forget this and you can throw this paper away. I am sorry I never met your father and in all the years with Rani, I never asked. It was not seemly. I raised you as my own because you *are* my own.' She stood up and looked at both of us firmly, her face rigid, a small tic starting at the lower end of her cheek. She poured more tea and told us to sit down again. Gabriel pressed my hand briefly and I answered with a slight pressure on his hand before letting it drop.

'We read your journals, Ammi. Those green journals you hid in the library? Gloria read some of the stories you wrote. They were good.'

The Magician's taut face stretched into a smile. 'They were terrible stories. All I did was rename the fairy-tale characters and put them in a modern setting with your names. If they'd been any good, I would have written them in English for you. I thought it would be something...'

'Something to remember you by.'

'Yes.'

'Why did you write them in Farsi?'

'For practice. And because I had no one to speak and read Farsi with – until Sohrab came. We read together and he gave me the idea that I could write some of the old stories for you and Gloria.' The Magician unlaced her fingers and sighed.

'Ammi, do you have anything of Rani's, anything I can look at?' I asked after a few minutes when the silence became heavy. I needed to see Rani's things, to see what else she had kept secret, what the Magician had not seen.

The Magician stood up and indicated we should follow her. We passed through the hall into a large room that looked out at distant houses clinging to the hillsides surrounding the town. Clouds careened their way across a freshly washed sky and somewhere outside trees creaked in the wind. The Magician waited for me to look at her before she spoke again.

'She had the biggest room in the house, with the best view. When she could no longer walk, she lay here and looked at the mountains. It gave her peace. She was in a lot of pain. I haven't touched anything. I was going to observe forty days of mourning, then…Now you are here. Please take whatever you like. I'll leave you alone.' The Magician left the room and Gabriel rubbed my cold hands.

Sari curtains swished in the breeze coming through partly open windows. A single bed in the centre of the room, piled high with embroidered pillows and cushions. The Magician's sketches – drawings of us as children – on the wall behind the bed. A sewing machine, similar to the Singer in the attic, pushed up against a wall and covered, a box beside it. Rani's fabric chest. I trawled through it as I had done as a child, when Rani watched me. Cotton, silk, lace, thread, rings, thimbles, buttons, boxes, obsessions. Neat squares, neat rectangles, neat hems, neat patches covering tiny flaws. A brown tablecloth with faded yellow and pink flowers. An embroidered butterfly on a plain pillowcase. White lace edging a pink hanky. Tiny buttons on the neck of a blouse she would never wear – pointless, useless, prettifying things. A life lived in defiance of the mess she had created. No letters, no more receipts. Nothing. Nothing to connect her to me. I closed the fabric chest and sat down on it, with my head in my hands, breathing in the musty smell of the brown tablecloth she was making on the day she disappeared.

When I lifted my eyes up to his, Gabriel extended his hand and hauled me into his embrace.

Forty-nine

Our flight to Perth was at fifteen minutes to midnight. We sat on the steel-framed black vinyl chairs and shifted uncomfortably. We didn't dare give up the seats because we had two hours to wait and the airport was packed. Already we had been asked to move our bags aside to accommodate a wheelchair occupied by a large lady and two small girls who asked if they could sit on our laps. Gabriel grinned when I told them I had an infectious disease that would make their noses fall off if they touched me. The children whispered something to their mother and moved some distance away. She glared at me and I was reminded of Meher. I swapped places with Gabriel so I didn't have to look at her and after a while she slept, a bubble of spit forming at the corner of her mouth, chins spread against her chest. The children sat near the chair and looked at us warily.

'Lady Karma will get you,' Gabriel whispered. 'What are the chances that your friend there with the kids will sit beside you on the long flight home? And they'll spill their drinks all over you?'

'I'll paint my nose pink and wriggle it at them. I may even shout in agony at intervals.'

'Your sister's right – you are quite anti-social. But funny.' Gabriel put an arm around me and kissed my nose.

∞

The Magician came with us to Mumbai and Marina clasped her close and cried for so long I couldn't bear to be in the same room, especially when the Magician reciprocated with hiccups and long sobs. I had acquired a distaste for public displays of grief. Grandfather Billy would have·been proud of my stoicism: 'Indians are a volatile people. This creates a great inconvenience for the Englishman and gives rise to the barbarous practice of excessive emotion and disobedience.'

'Ask her to come back with us,' Gabriel urged quietly. 'She's waiting for you to ask.'

'I can't. Her instincts as a mother are flawed. I don't want her around Bahareh. She doesn't even believe the sordidness of my birth. She's still in denial.'

'Hannah.'

'What?'

'It's not your call. And it's not her fault. She's still your mother – the only one you have. Are you going to say something? You've been amazing so far – don't spoil it.'

We said goodbye at Marina's door. 'No need to come to the airport, Ammi,' I said, waving away her protests. 'You haven't been to Mumbai in years and you'll get lost on your way back.'

'Hannah, you've grown into a bossy young lady and I can't argue with you.' The Magician's smile didn't reach her eyes, but I swept her into my embrace as if she'd said something endearing. We held each other for a long time and when we parted we were both dry-eyed. She pressed something cold and round into my hand and said, 'I want you to have this.' I looked down at the thick yellow bangle she used to wear and drew back.

'I can't take this. I'll give it to Gloria.'

'No. It's yours. It's Rani's. She gave it to me when you were born. It belonged to her mother.'

At last.

Something my birth mother had intended for me. So why did this gold bangle, symbol of happy days spent hanging around the kitchen with the Magician, look like a curled cobra in my palm? Why did I want to drop it and wash my hands vigorously?

'Put it on,' the Magician said, squeezing my right hand and preparing to slide the bangle on.

'Not just yet, Ammi. My wrists aren't as soft as yours. I'll need soap and water to slide it on. I'll do it later. Lots of time to kill at the airport.'

'As you wish.' The Magician stepped back and I dropped the bangle into my bag.

'Ammi, you know you're welcome. Always. You have two homes in Perth if you ever want to come, and a granddaughter to dandle on your knee, so think about it?'

The Magician's eyes filled and she smiled. 'Some day, yes. My mountain home suits me – it must be a race memory. My parents came from Azerbaijan, you know.'

'*O Sohrab, an unquiet heart is thine! Canst thou not rest among the Tartar chiefs, And share the battle's common chance with us Who love thee?*'

'Oh, very good, Maryam, you remember it well. Yes, and since I'll never go there I'll make do with Shimla. Come and visit me again. With your children and husband. May God protect you both.'

'I mean it, Ammi, come back with us – it'll be odd at first but we're all adults now and not scared any more. There's nothing for you here. How can you not want to see Bahareh? Please, at least think about it. We love you. We've missed you. Share the battle's common chance with us and read that dreadful poem to us again.'

This time there was no awkwardness in the Magician's embrace. We fitted comfortably around each other. Her softness adjusted to all my sharp angles and I thought of the times she had held me, every touch a promise, every breath a reminder, every kiss an affirmation. She pulled out a large white hanky and wiped my face gently, as she used to after a fight with Gloria or a thump from Warren.

∞

I took Rani's circle of gold out of my handbag and slipped it on my right wrist. It went on easily.

'Very flash,' said Gabriel. 'It looks nice. Is it old?'

'I suppose. I don't even know how old Rani was when she died. And if this belonged to her mother, the Historian's mother, it must be old. My grandparents died before any of us came along. It was an odd relationship, according to the Historian, when he talked about them, which wasn't often. His father named him and brought him up Catholic, while Rani was named by her Indian mother and brought up Hindu. Grandfather William believed in religious democracy, apparently.'

'And you? What do you believe?' Gabriel drew my head down on his shoulder.

'I believe I love you.'

'That's an excellent response. Just you remember that.'

'Gabriel?'

'Hmm?'

'Am I normal? An aberration? A monster? Lovable?'

'No one could accuse you of being normal, Hannah. How you came to be here isn't important. What you're going to do next is. And I'd like to always be part of that, if you'll let me. Many rivers to cross and all that.'

The first call for boarding crackled through in three languages and we stood up, gathered our bags and backpacks, and joined the queue waiting to board Singapore Airlines Flight 294.

Fifty

My brothers were there, behind tubular metal barriers at Perth Airport, and the Historian and Gloria with Bahareh, arms outstretched, scanning our faces, unease filtering through cracks in their smiles. I put down my backpack and swung Bahareh off the ground and into my arms. She looked surprised, then smiled and fastened both arms around my neck.

'Marcie,' she said. 'Hannah Marcie Mummy.'

'You've learned to say my name, you clever girl.'

'She learned to huff while you were gone,' Gloria said, folding us both into her embrace. 'Makes a change from Anna Marcie, thank God. Oh, it's good to have you back.'

The Historian tapped us and put an arm around me when I turned, his eyes searching mine. Clive and Warren stepped up and kissed me on the cheek and thumped Gabriel's back.

'Indian family reunion,' I said to Gabriel. 'We should go away more often. Don't any of you work?'

They laughed and placed their bodies between mine and the Historian's, picked up our bags and herded us through the swishing doors and out into the squint-inducing blue of a Perth afternoon. Clive led us to his car and the rest piled into the Historian's gold Land Cruiser.

'They're all coming over to yours,' Clive said over his shoulder as he stopped to slip a ticket into the boom gate. 'Aunty Frankie and the girls are already there. Sorry if you thought you could come in quietly without anyone noticing.'

I said nothing, watching the cars weave around the roundabouts and speed up on the straight road towards the Tonkin Highway. Tall trees, a flutter of cockatoos and the sky a blank canvas stretched overhead, the rumble of planes taking off and the Seekers playing 'Red Rubber Ball' on the radio. No scooters, rickshaws, children tapping at car windows; one mother dead, another diminished, a father more firmly attached to my blood than ever before.

And a man twisting around from the front seat to check on me – a man with laughing eyes and warm hands, a man whose heartbeat I held, who looked as if he had something important to ask me.

'Yes,' I said to Gabriel. 'Whatever it is, the answer is yes.'

NOTES

The poem 'Sohrab and Rustum' by Matthew Arnold is quoted throughout the manuscript. The versions of the poem I worked with come from *Three Narrative Poems*, edited by J. Fuste (Student Stores, Delhi, 1973) as well as online at <www.poetryfoundation. org/poem/172860>.

On the first page, the sentence, 'violent insane lunatics subject to maniacal paroxysms of fury' was inspired by the description of an asylum found in *The History of Deolali Cantonment (1867–1947)*, compiled by P.N. Jaywant. I am grateful to Brigadier Jaywant for lending me a copy of his book when I visited Deolali in 2014.

Hannah's 'lush' words come from *Liberalism and Indian Politics: 1872–1922* by R.J. Moore (Foundations of Modern History series, Edward Arnold, London, 1966) as well as *Peoples and Problems of India* by Sir T.W. Holderness (Williams and Norgate, London, 1911). The references to conquistadors, and Lord Dalhousie in particular, also come from this volume.

Grandfather William's journal entries had their foundations in *A General History of England, 1688–1832* by W.A. Barker, G.R. St Aubyn and R.L. Ollard (A. & C. Black, London, 1952). I referred to this volume for language rather than history, primarily because of its descriptions of Indians as 'natives' and the British as 'masters'. I wanted Grandfather William to be a little discerning in his acceptance of the 'valour and genius' of the British in India.

For access to the library at the Indian Institute of Advanced Studies in Shimla, I am deeply indebted to Professor Pankaj Singh and her amazing team at Himachal Pradesh University.

The song lyrics in Chapter 19 come from The Jesus and Mary Chain's 'Psychocandy' and 'Darklands'.

ACKNOWLEDGEMENTS

This novel was written as part of my PhD thesis at Edith Cowan University. I thank my principal supervisor, Dr Ffion Murphy, for her professional courtesy, patience and steady commitment to my project over the four years of my candidature. I also thank Dr Marcella Polain, my associate supervisor, for her insightful reading of the finished manuscript as well as her gentle comments at the end of a stressful year.

To my fabulous colleagues at ECU, Brenda Downing, Kylie Stevenson, Louise Helfgott, Lauren Marsh and Kim Coull, who shared my journey with joy and boundless generosity, my love. To Marilyn Metta and Amanda Curtin, who told me, at different times, to believe in the power of 'unruly stories', my thanks. To the OWLS, Liana, Karen and Cecily, who were the first to meet Hannah and the Historian and the first to tell me to 'surrender', my gratitude.

A special thanks to Professor Pankaj Singh in Shimla for showing me *the* old library and inviting me into the lives of her colleagues and students while being the nicest, most knowledgeable and gracious of hosts during my residency at Himachal Pradesh University.

My husband, Mike, and my children, Sabah and Matt, laughed at me when I lost perspective, and gave me information on router bits, marri trees and dodgy cars. Additionally, Mike ensured a steady supply of coffee, sympathy, books and *Star Trek* re-runs. To Kylie and Gerard, my thanks for sharing your lives and Charlotte with me. To John, my life is richer for your gentle presence.

My sincere thanks and heartfelt gratitude to the Reading Women, who cannot be named and whose forthright discussions, laughter and opinions remain with me, and without whom the second part of this book would have been so much harder to write. My love and thanks to Mum and Dad and my lovely sister, whose faith in me never wavered.

My sincere gratitude and thanks to Nicola Young for her editing suggestions and astute observations while preparing this novel for publication. Finally, without Terri-ann White and her fabulous team at UWA Publishing, this novel would still be just a manuscript. My most heartfelt thanks.

www.ingramcontent.com/pod-product-compliance
Lightning Source LLC
Chambersburg PA
CBHW020400030726
47496CB00007B/2235